The Forgotten Spell

Louisa Dent

Wizard Books

Published in the UK in 2006 by Wizard Books,
an imprint of Icon Books Ltd.,
The Old Dairy, Brook Road, Thriplow,
Cambridge SG8 7RG
email: wizard@iconbooks.co.uk
www.iconbooks.co.uk/wizard

Sold in the UK, Europe, South Africa
and Asia by Faber and Faber Ltd.,
3 Queen Square, London WC1N 3AU
or their agents

Distributed in the UK, Europe, South Africa
and Asia by TBS Ltd., Frating Distribution Centre,
Colchester Road, Frating Green, Colchester CO7 7DW

Published in Australia in 2006
by Allen & Unwin Pty. Ltd.,
PO Box 8500, 83 Alexander Street,
Crows Nest, NSW 2065

Distributed in Canada by
Penguin Books Canada,
90 Eglinton Avenue East, Suite 700,
Toronto, Ontario M4P 2Y3

ISBN-10: 1-84046-731-2
ISBN-13: 978-1-840467-31-4

Typesetting by Hands Fotoset

Printed and bound in the UK by Clays of Bungay

INTRODUCTION

You are about to enter into the strange and dangerous world of the faeries. Sometimes called the Fey, they are a vast population of creatures that inhabit a world out of reach of mortals. It is a world of forgotten forests and high mountain ranges, of black oceans and uncharted shorelines. A world of cities, ancient and unmapped, filled with language and culture and cursed gossip drifting between the rain-soaked streets. Here live faeries as large as men and as small as toads. There are clans of dwarves and gangs of goblins. There are trolls, leprechauns, dryads, sithes, bruinies, mirfolk, gnomes, lughtins and hags. There are other creatures, too, which have no names and live deep in the wildernesses, never to be seen or heard.

It all lies just beyond the *pale*, the space between night and day, sleep and waking, shadows and light.

There are few who can find it and fewer still who can return. The mortal is no match for the magic of the Fey. Yet your quest will take you into this world, to one of the most evil and despised cities of the faery: the city of Suidemor. Here you must be prepared to test your courage, strength and wit against the myriad of evil foes that await you. Will you survive?

SUIDEMOR

Suidemor lies on the southern shores of a vast continent. It is the last outpost of all the civilised kingdoms of the Elder Fey – the race of faeries who have risen to power by virtue of their great cities and castles, built with a powerful magic craft, the secrets of which they keep hidden from all.

Suidemor has been all but forgotten by the Elder Fey rulers of the North. Isolated by wild and uncharted oceans, the city's edifices are beaten by wind and rain, snow and hail. It is always cold and always miserable. Here live faeries who have come from better cities, prouder cities, bringing with them cauldrons and curses and unsettled arguments. By the light of the southern moon they trade in crafts and magic, and walk upon the ancient stones talking of dark deeds from under their hoods.

THE MORTAL WORLD

Living in the world of men, you are the only child of the mortal woman Eleanore. Though she is loving and kind, your mother is perpetually sad, doomed to forever mourn the disappearence of your father, who vanished without a trace on the very day you were born. Except for this one mystery, your life has been quite ordinary and unremarkable. You know nothing of the world of the faery or the troubles of Suidemor. Yet all that is about to change, for even as you sleep safely in your bed, there are those who are plotting to destroy you. As your 13th birthday arrives, unseen forces gather beyond the pale, preparing you for a quest that may cost your life.

HOW TO READ THIS BOOK

Like the faeries, this book is not friendly. You will have to decide which way to go, which fey to trust and, ultimately, how the story ends. Make your choices by following the instructions at the end of each paragraph. Choose wisely, because once you have turned the page, you will not be able to go back!

CASTING SPELLS

The world of the faeries is magical, and there are many different types of magic, from the powerful and ancient systems of Elder Magic and Witcherie, to the more simple crafts of earth magic, spirit magic and conjuring. To survive, you will need at least a basic range of skills and spells. You will have to wait until you find your spellbook in the journey before you can start using magic. When you find the book, you will be given special instructions on how to use it. Until then, you are unprotected and very vulnerable to the powers of the fey, so beware!

KEEPING RECORDS

Carry a pencil with you, as you will need to note any valuable information and items that you find along the way. For this purpose, you may use the adventure sheet on page 8.

The common currency in Suidemor is the *geld*, available in copper, silver and gold. At times you may have to calculate your own change. You will find that one silver equals five coppers, and one gold equals twenty coppers. Keep a record of the geld you find or earn, as you will need to pay for some things. This is, after all, a city busy with trade.

SOLVING PUZZLES

The creatures you will meet are secretive, and their secrets are often bound in puzzles. Instructions will be given when you come across a puzzle. You may pick up clues along the way that will help you solve puzzles, so note anything down that you think may be important.

If you cannot solve a puzzle, you may use the Puzzle Solver at the back of the book. You will not usually be reminded of this option – you may simply turn to it when you need it. But beware – by using the Puzzle Solver, you are relying on intuition and luck. Because luck has a way of running out, you may use this page no more than *three times* during your adventure.

A FINAL WORD

Though you will be able to wield magic, your wit is your greatest weapon. Take heed of all you see and hear and keep your courage, for you will need it to find your way through this story, in the quest to find…

The Forgotten Spell.

Turn to paragraph 1 to begin your adventure…

ADVENTURE SHEET

GELD RECORD

5 Coppers=1 Silver 20 Coppers=1 Gold 4 Silver=1 Gold

POSSESSIONS

CURSINGS and BLESSINGS

CALCULATIONS

CLUES

NEW SPELLS

THE FORGOTTEN SPELL

1

It is your 13th birthday, this dreary winter's day on which you hurry home from school. Your shoes splash in puddles as you criss-cross the streets of the large, grey city where you live. Picking a well-worn path under the eaves of the buildings, you come to the doorway of a gloomy, many-storied block of flats. You bound up the stairway, three at a time, passing Mrs Clement who is descending, and who shakes her black umbrella disapprovingly at you.

'You watch out for your mother – I've a bad feeling about today!' she calls out.

You ignore her, quickly reaching the landing of the top floor flat.

You retrieve your key from the pocket of your school uniform, but as you insert it, you are surprised to find that the door is already unlocked. You pause, catching your breath. You mother never leaves the door unlocked. On the doormat you notice something else that's odd – a single, black feather has fallen there.

Stepping over the feather, you open the door. Inside, the flat is dark and smells of oil paint and turpentine, and is filled with a clutter of canvases. Your mother is nowhere to be seen, and she has likely retired to her workshop to paint. Dumping your schoolbag on the floor, you notice that she has left some coins and a scribbled note for you on the kitchen table. The note reads:

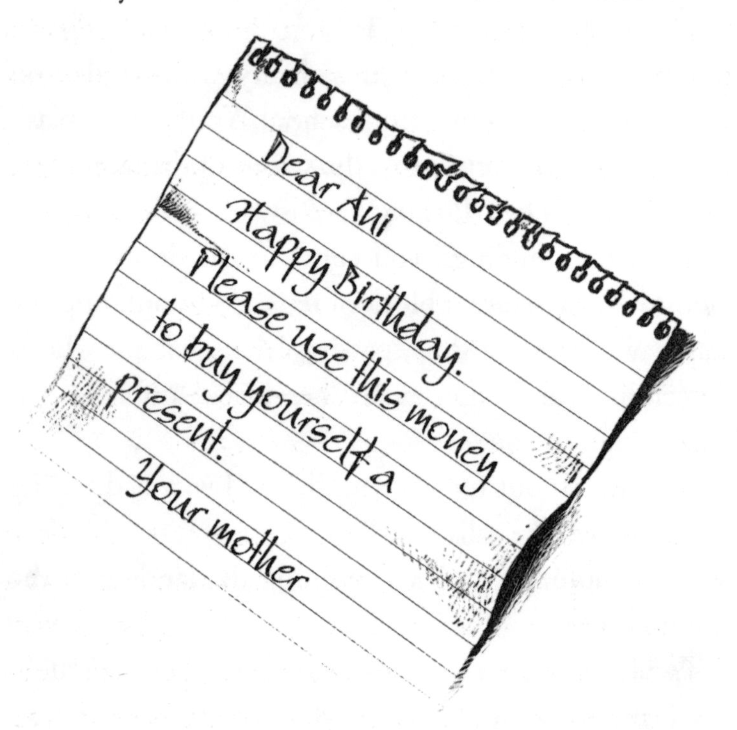
Dear Ani
Happy Birthday.
Please use this money
to buy yourself a
present.
Your mother

You count the coins, thinking happily of the things you can buy, when suddenly you hear voices, raised and angry, coming from your mother's workshop. You creep across the darkened flat towards the workshop door.

'The child is not here … there is no person of that name!' you hear your mother say.

The door is ajar. Through the crack you see the shadow of a man against the water-stained wall. You strain to hear his words, spoken in a strange accent.

'Mortals can nun change this child's destiny. I, Olcrada, alone have the power,' he says.

His shadow grows larger. From his shoulder blades you see two wings slowly spreading, their shadows creeping across the wall like bloodstains.

'Anivad belongs to me now,' says the stranger. He continues in a language you have never heard before:

Begetten sicklie wyth myrred plegm,
Airedd byen tænted wind
Fouledd breath en blækenedd blod
Reepen sowen ere het life

Your mother cries out. Alarmed, you open the door wide to see her kneeling in the chalkdust and pencil shavings of her workshop floor, grasping at her throat. The stranger turns swiftly to meet you, his gaze burning, the pair of great wings glimmering behind him. Sitting on his forearm is a black, sleek-feathered crow. The man advances towards you in three strides.

'Ye – ye have the Elder Fey sight,' he hisses, 'Now it will be your curse.' He speaks another string of strange words.

You are suddenly thrown against the wall, crashing into the shelves of paint and brushes. Jars smash on the ground. The stranger holds you in his gaze as you try to get to your feet. You slump back to the floor instead.

The coins clutched in your hand are scattered like marbles.

'Happy Birthday,' mocks the stranger. 'Ye will not live to see another.'

A wave of nausea washes over you. The feeling is like death itself. You try to inch towards your mother, but the effort collapses you. You are powerless to stop yourself being taken by the blackness.

Turn to **19**.

2

You open the jar of salve-all cream and apply some gently to the pigeon's wounded wing. The salve-all cream will restore the bird's vitality. You may meet this creature again in another part of your journey, perhaps in book two or three. If you do, turn to **99** in that book to receive its help in return. Make a note of this clue, and turn to **168** to enter the tavern.

3

The candle is made of beeswax. The merchant tells you that to light it, you need only blow on the wick.

Return to **258**.

4

You fumble in your satchel for the vivifying elixir. You quickly unstopper the bottle and take a sip of the liquid.

Your body is wracked by a chill. When you open your eyes, you see the faces of faeries gathered around you. Pucker is pointing at you with glee, laughing at your dilemma.

'Can nun hold the spirut!' you hear someone yell.

You pull yourself quickly to your feet. You glance around for support, but there is none. It seems to be time to take your leave.

Turn to **186**.

5

You shoulder your satchel and turn to leave the bakery, feeling the glare of the proprietor and his solitary customer on your back. As you push open the door, a hunched figure steps into the doorway to meet you. She is a hag, her face partly concealed beneath a dirty hood. She glares at you with a puffy blood-stained eye and catches your wrist with her icy hand.

''Tis œnly Pearlie!' she rasps at you.

Have you seen Pearlie in another shop? If so, turn to **148**. If not, turn to **152**.

6

You crawl towards the wreckage. The driver's seat and steering wheel are visible, though horribly buckled. Your heart lurches as you make out the form of the greeper's body, crushed between the crumpled metal and the wall. His head is twisted away from you and you are grateful not to have to see his face. You find his wrist and check his pulse, sure that he must be dead. But his hand suddenly clutches yours, and you are shocked to hear him speak, his voice weak.

'The flames … The flames have saved ye. The oobanata … can nun … abide suche fires. Now go quickly – down Muncaster Alley!'

With these words his hand goes limp. You check his

pulse. There is nothing. He is dead. A wave of nausea washes over you.

You look around wildly for Muncaster Alley. The only alley you can see is across the courtyard, which is now thick with smoke and flames. Choking from the foul air and hot wind, you stumble from the wreckage and dash across the courtyard.

Turn to **11**.

7

You sit on the damp floor, fighting your growing panic. There is a dead silence all about you. Minutes pass, becoming hours. No one comes for you. Nothing happens.

Will you try to climb the walls (turn to **29**), or shout for help (turn to **64**)?

8

At the same moment that you realise what the number is, the graffiti transforms to reveal a message slashed across the wall:

When Elder Fey do close their eyes
Okrada from their blood will rise

The message is a chilling one.

Return now to your previous paragraph number.

9

He is Hensoi the bonsai herbalist. He is happy to show you his collection of bonsai trees, each of which takes thousands of years to grow. Suitably impressed, you marvel at the little trees. Hensoi explains how each one produces a different beneficial fruit, seed, leaf or root to be used for the treatment of ailments or as ingredients for magic. He also sells a range of common herbs for cooking. While most of the wares are too expensive

Bonsai Herbes:
3 copper geld per bagg

geldwort seeds
'for riches and luck'

feverfew flowers
'for poisons and minor ailments'

ghoul's thistle
'for spirut curses'

for you, Hensoi shows you the last of his seasonal specials.

Buy as many herbs as you want, or can afford, and turn to **39**. If you don't want to buy anything, turn to **102**.

10

You tell the drunk you don't want his help and push roughly past him to get to the door. But as you reach for the handle, you find your hand has gone numb and is unable to grip anything. You try with the other hand, but you find it is the same. You grope clumsily at the handle, feeling more and more silly and a little panicked. The drunk has cast a spell on you! He appears beside you, his face inches from your own.

'Suche a symple spell, and yet ye be helpless. Yeour magick be yer only defence, and ye must learn to usen it.'

With these words, he turns and disappears through the crowd. As the feeling returns to your hands, you realise that he is right.

You catch up with him through the jostling crowd. He leads you away from the door towards a table at the back of the tavern where the light from the oil lamps does not reach. He offers you a chair at the table, cluttered by empty drinking glasses. You slide into the chair, clutching your satchel close.

Turn to **140**.

11

You escape into the alleyway, which is narrow and filled with bits of junk you are forced to stumble around and climb over. You are most thankful to find it is not a dead end. Running blindly, you are soon lost in a labyrinth of streets and laneways. Your shoes slip on the rain-soaked stones and rotting leaves. Damp air penetrates your clothes. In darkened corners you catch glimpses of creatures hunched over piles of garbage, their goblin-esque faces leering. Beautiful beings with wings flit between the shadows of the buildings. None of these do you recognise as human.

You run to exhaustion, brought to a stop at last in the darkest, dingiest alleyway you can find. Even here you do not feel safe. Between the buildings, a sliver of sky provides vantage enough for the crows, should they seek you. You investigate the alleyway for shelter. While the piles of rubbish do not look too appealing and the alleyway itself is a dead-end, you notice a window and glass-panelled door at the alley's end, through which the

inviting glow of lantern-light can be seen. Above the door you read the sign:

Garda Grye's
Parchements & Bookes
Bought & Sold

You peer through the grime-covered glass of the window, but can make out only some drapes of a stained material and a glimpse of bookshelves beyond. You hear the sound of keys rattling. In the next moment, the shop door flies opens. An old woman with a face like crumpled parchment stares out at you, her wiry white hair held close under a woollen cap. She breathes steam in the cold air as she casts her eye over the alleyway.

'The back entrance, eh? Nun be using this entrance for nigh on a hundred years.' She sniffs, taking in your dishevelled clothes and satchel and muttering, 'Trouble, trouble, why must troubles always come to my door…'

The old woman makes a clucking sound between her teeth, darts a look down the alley, and ushers you in without a word.

Turn to 76.

12

On closer inspection, you see that the box contains not matches, but tiny candles. The advertising on the box suggests that the 'match candles' can be lit by simply blowing on their wicks.

There is one match candle left in the box. Make a note of your new possession and return to your previous paragraph number.

13

You wave at the tram and it comes to a grinding halt on the tracks. Steam billows up behind it. You catch the handrail and pull yourself aboard.

Stepping into the carriage, you are immediately filled with a sense of foreboding. The tram is filled with passengers, but there is something strange about them. They turn to stare at you with hollow eyes and gaunt cheeks, their bones showing under translucent skins. None of them speak. The bell rings and you feel the gears grinding underfoot as the machine begins to move.

Do you want to try jumping off the tram (turn to **30**), or stay on board (turn to **103**)?

14

You lay down on the ground, your head resting under a large bloom. Its petals are enormous, the stamen heavy with nectar. You reach out to touch the flower. The petals immediately shrivel and change colour from yellow to violet, while the thick, green stems of the vine begin to creep towards you! You get to your feet, vaguely alarmed. A tendril lashes out at you, stinging your arms.

You will have to use magic to escape the frapella vines. Cast your spell now.

15

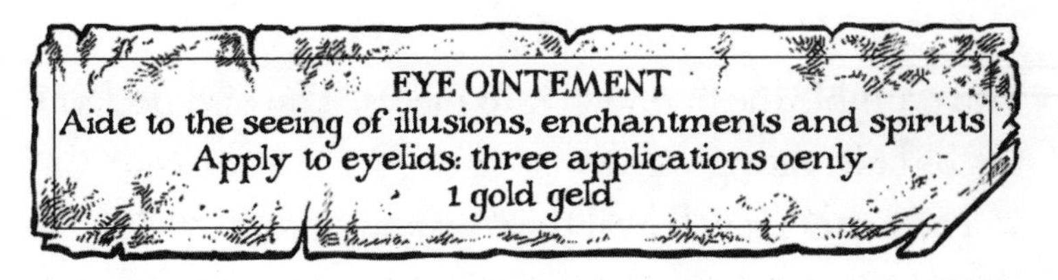

16

Your climb is painstakingly slow as you try to grip the stones. Some are slimy, some are sharp and cut your fingers. The nettles quiver beside you, ready to lash out. You are shaking from exhaustion and fear by the time your fingers find the edge of the hole. With a last ounce of strength, you heave yourself into the gaping space. Looking about, you muffle an urge to scream – peering at you is a pale, fleshy face and a pair of blood-shot, luminous eyes. The creature motions you with its dirt-stained hands, and disappears into the darkness. Breathing hard, you follow.

Turn to 55.

17

You crumble the bannoch into pieces. The bird pecks at the biscuit, eating warily.

The bannoch will heal the bird and restore its vitality. You may meet this creature again in another part of your journey, perhaps in book two or three. If you do, turn to **99** in that book to receive its help in return. Make a note of this clue, and turn to **168** to enter the tavern.

18

You ask the doctor if he has heard of the Forgotten Spell. He holds you under his cool regard.

'Ye ask of dangerous thinges, fer it be a spell of ancient Witcherie magick. But this be a place of medicinnes, nun of questions. Make known your ailment or purchase, or be gone.'

Would you like to buy something now (turn to **58**), or take your leave (turn to **226**)?

19

When you wake, it is so dark that for a moment you think it is the middle of the night. But you are not in your bed and a sliver of cold light from above reveals stone walls rising high about you. Your limbs ache and your clothes are smeared with dirt. How long have you been here? You cannot tell. The memory of your mother's scream floods back to you, and of the man with wings who called himself Olcrada. You shudder violently, your stomach heaving. You are a prisoner, trapped in a cell barely an arm's span in width. The floor is sealed and there are no doors. The boards on which you stand are omniously worn, as though many a creature has paced upon them. Your only hope of escape seems to be a window high above, covered with a steel grating. Yet the rough stones that imprison you provide treacherous footholds, covered in slime and lichen and strange nettle-like plants that grow between the cracks.

Will you sit tight and see if someone comes for you (turn to 7), shout for help (turn to **105**) or try to climb the walls (turn to 29)?

20

You retrieve the miniature compass from your satchel. Behind the glass a needle quivers, clearly indicating the way ahead.

Ignoring the lane to your right, you continue on, soon arriving at another junction. This time the needle indicates to turn left. Looking to the left, you see another junction some distance away. Looking to the right, the lane is a apparent dead-end, but for the indistinct shape of a door, partly hidden behind the rose brambles.

Will you continue to follow the compass (turn to **195**), or try the door (turn to **279**)?

21

The door of the shop is set into what appears to be the enormous trunk of a tree. Above the shop, bare branches arch over the pavement in an entanglement which serves as a natural awning. Set on either side of the door are windows of green-stained glass.

You push open the door and step into a room of refracted green light. The sound of trickling water greets you. In the centre of the shop is a pond and a small fountain, filled with lilies and tiny ferns. At the back of the shop, an archway leads into a small glass-house. Here the light is even and bright, pouring in through the roof and spilling onto a collection of miniature trees. A faery hovers over the trees, tilting a watering can and soaking the plants with a cascade of droplets. His clothes are made of leaves and his wings are many shades of green. He turns to look at you with soft, unblinking eyes.

Turn to **9**.

22

There is nothing you can do to stop from falling into a deep sleep.

Turn to **32**.

23

You offer the dwarf a drink. With a grunt that indicates some interest in you, he signals for a passing barmaid. She wears a stained apron over her scrawny frame and carries a tray of drinks. The dwarf grabs her wrist.

'Bladderwracks fer the table,' he leers at her.

The barmaid sets two goblet-shaped glasses of dark liquid before you. She is asking two coppers a piece for the drinks.

Pay the barmaid if you can, and turn to **265**. If you cannot pay for the drinks, turn to **69**.

24

You open the jar of ointment and smear a little on each eyelid. When you open your eyes, you are amazed to see that the treats which looked good now look sickly and stale. The very sticky Blas Buns are at least a week old and filled with a rancid sauce, while the Lucky Dips are bitter and spoiled. The bread, toffee apples and biscuits are all good choices, and their numbers are as follows:

Fallaid bread: **235** (1 gold geld)
Toffee apples: **202** (2 copper geld)
Bannoch biscuit: **145** (1 copper geld)

Remember you only had enough eye ointment for three applications. Make a note that you have used the ointment and then turn to the numbers above if you wish to make a purchase. If you have no money or you don't want to purchase anything, turn to **5**.

25

You sneak up to the tree. There are coins everywhere! You begin to gather them up, but you are soon distracted by the harsh cry of a bird. You look up to see a pair of magpies circling in the sky above. As you hastily cram the coins into your pockets, one of the birds swoops from the sky, coming straight towards you!

You will have to cast a spell immediately.

26

Defeated, you carve your triangle. Effie uses both fists to plunge her knife into the wood of the winning square.

'Effie's table,' she says, shadowing you with her bulk as she leans forward. The knife glints menacingly. 'Paye Effie,' she says.

Effie will accept as payment either your entire bag of coins or an entire bag of toffee apples. If you have either of these items and you want to pay her, make a note of your loss and turn to 234. If you can't pay Effie, or you don't want to, turn to 223.

27

You search your satchel for something to give Cyleric. As you do, you realise that all of your belongings are gone, save for your spellbook!

'Thief!' you accuse him.

Cyleric grins sourly and opens his cloak. He lays on the table your possessions, every one of them.

'A lesson, feyling,' he says, wagging his finger at you as you angrily gather up your belongings.

With a parting promise that you will not forget his help – nor his ill deeds – you take your leave.

Turn to **50**.

28

You carve your triangle roughly in the wood. Effie examines your move and carves a cross in reply. There is only one move you can make to stop her from getting three crosses in a row.

Turn to 325.

29

You grab hold of a stone. The nearby nettles quiver, turning their spikey heads towards you.

Will you persist in climbing this part of the wall (turn to **125**), or try another stone (turn to **70**)?

30

As you prepare to jump from the doorway the nearby passengers gather around you, their ghostly arms outstretched. One of them strokes the fabric of your cloak. You beat off the hand in a panic, only to find the long pale fingers curling around your wrist.

Do you have any ghoul's thistle? If so, turn to 166. If not you will have to use your magic to escape the tram, or you will be doomed to ride the #13 with the Unseelies for eternity. Choose your spell carefully, as you have only enough time to cast one.

31

You pull out the book for the Warlock. The priest takes it, feeling the cover with his hands.

'This be a goodlie gift, indeed. In return, I shall tell ye this: the path to the Arch Warlock be always opened to those who be strong of heart, but it be protected by many devyces to fool the wycked. Be nun tempted along yer path, nun by geld, nor restful places, nor even cries for help. Climb nun the walls. Sing a song if you must walk under the frapella vines. This be the waye ye will find the Warlock's home.'

He gestures towards the door at the top of the steps.

You gaze at the door. It is twice your height at least, held shut by an iron latch. At the priest's invitation, you climb the worn steps and pull the latch.

Make a note of the priest's clues. If you come to the frapella vines, add 10 to the paragraph number to pass under them safely. Turn to **83**.

32

When you come to your senses, you find yourself cramped and lying in a darkened corner. Music and laughter penetrate your dulled hearing. You recognise the sounds of lunchtime at the Brackenrose Arms and realise with some relief that you have not been unconscious for long. As you try to sit up, you remember your satchel. You grope about frantically, checking under the tables and chairs for your lost property, even as you acknowledge with a sinking heart that finding your valuables in a place like this would be nothing short of miraculous.

'Ye be fossicking for this?' you hear someone say. You look up to see a bleary-eyed and nobble-faced faery sitting at a nearby table, his wings covering his shoulders like drapes of worn, silken material. On the table is your satchel. You find yourself held in the gaze of his bloodshot eyes.

'Elder Fey, be ye not?' he says. 'Though ye be nun initiated … 'Tis strange and rare, though it be possible in these darkened dayes … Have ye trouble with magick? Inabilitie to casten spells?' He glances around secretively, then whispers, 'Buye me a drinkun and I will initiate ye in arte of Elder magick.' You begin to say that you don't have any geld, but he raises his finger to silence you. 'Whenne we be finished, ye wyll not need geld,' he says with a wink.

Turn to **140**.

33

The merchant pulls more candles from his coat, waving them under your nose and expounding their magnificent properties in a raised voice. You shake your head at his offerings, but he is not deterred. The exchange is beginning to draw the attention of nearby passengers. You realise you are going to have to rid yourself of the merchant.

You may either cast a spell to be rid of him or disembark from the tram (turn to **151**).

34

You land on the cobblestones, grazing your hands. At least you are alive, you acknowledge grimly, as you pick yourself up and hobble to the pavement.

Turn to **109**.

35

'Thirty-five,' you say out loud. The lines carved on the table shine with clarity, while Cyleric regards you with solemn pleasure.

'Wyth this insight and utterance, ye have passed the initiation. Your spells will work and ye be free to learn your arte, the power of which is becweathed ye by the Ordughadh of the Elder Fey.' Cyleric inclines his head to you in acknowledgement of your achievement.

In the tavern, the music has stopped and time has passed. The lunchtime patrons have dwindled to a few grisly regulars. Barmaids clean the tables of broken glass and spilt drink. Like you, Cyleric has become aware of the surroundings. Indeed, he seems to dwindle to his former presence as he lowers his voice to a whisper.

'It will soon be time for ye to leave, for there be those who already have noticed our comradeship. These be dark times for the Elder Fey, fer we be a dying race and there be many who wish to take our place. But before ye go, we must test your cræft.' He grins. 'For this, I wyll teach ye a spell of mine own devyce.'

You watch as he proceeds to empty the pockets of his cloak. All manner of strange paraphernalia are laid on the table: rings and stones, dead insects, pieces of parchment and little jars. He sifts through the pile and extracts five grey feathers.

'First, ye be needing a set of thinges of common shape,' he says, cupping the feathers in his hand. 'The wyrd of the spell be "geld", and the number be 24.' Cyleric gives you the feathers. 'Now utter the wyrd,' he instructs.

Make a note of the spell. To cast the spell, add the number of the spell to this paragraph number and turn to the result now.

13
Schedule
dayes
everie other daye
everie full moon
some dayes
and again
4 O'Clock
nyght~time
twilight

36

The hand grasps at your offering with its finger and thumb, and snatches it away beneath the rags.

'Blessen ye, fey,' rasps the voice.

The hand reappears, parting the folds of smelly material. You step back, startled to see a handful of dried leaves released from the rags. One of them lands at your feet and you recognise it as a shamrock – the lucky four-leafed clover. The rest of the leaves are blown about by the wind, soon disappearing. You see that the creature has once again hidden itself under the rags. Quickly pocketing the shamrock, you hurry on your way.

Make a note that you are carrying a shamrock and turn to 222.

37

You give the copper coin to the time-keeper. She points to the street with her spoon.

'I'll give ye the time! It be the now!'

She shrieks gleefully and slams the door in your face. You glance up the street to see another dilapidated machine rumbling towards you.

Do you want to catch the tram (turn to **13**), or continue on foot (turn to **109**)?

38

You try to wrench your wrist free. The dwarf watches you struggle, amused by your efforts, then he suddenly releases his grip and sends you sprawling backwards into the next table. Onlookers laugh and whistle.

'Next time ye will mind yer plæce, feyling,' sneers the dwarf.

With as much dignity as you can muster, you get to your feet and slip into the crowd, ignoring the jeers behind you.

Turn to **186**.

39

As you tuck your purchases safely in your satchel, you hear the shop bell tinkling. The miniature trees shiver in a draught of cold air, and a pungent smell reaches your nose. Hensoi peers into the shop.

'Who be in my shoppe?' he calls out nervously.

You see a hunched figure dressed in rags standing near the doorway.

''Tis oenly Pearlie, little fey, in need of some goodlie herbes,' a rasping voice replies.

Have you seen Pearlie in another shop? If so, turn to **120**. If not, turn to **79**.

40

The compass is encased in a gold locket. Turning the locket over, you see the following words inscribed on the back:

Whyche waye wyll ye go?
Point me and ye wyll know

The compass looks to be of some value, as well as potentially useful.

Return to 258.

41

You wend your way to a quieter part of the bar, where you hope to remain inconspicuous. As you survey the concoctions on display, you feel a hot breath on your neck. You turn quickly to meet the bloodshot eyes of a young faery who looks about your age.

'Fancie a drink?' he grins at you.

At the same time a barmaid with arms as thin as straws arrives to serve, her lips set in an expression of acquired hopelessness.

Will you accept a drink from the faery (turn to **92**), or decline his offer (turn to **119**)?

very sweet very sticky
BLAS BUNS
134
LUCKIE DIPS
224
TOFFEE APPLES
202
FALLIARD
BREAD
235
BANNOCH
145

42

You insert the key. The tumblers click. You unlatch the door and pull it open upon a scene of horror. The Elemental crouches before you, haunches glistening with sweat. Before you have time to react, icy breath envelops you as the creature attacks. Talons tear into your flesh. A triumphant shriek fills the air, accompanied by your final valiant cry as you slump to the ground, the smell of your own blood and death rising about you, before a curtain of darkness is pulled over your eyes ...

Turn to 332.

43

You enter the shop and are greeted by warm air from the ovens and a myriad of delicious smells. The chairs and tables are occupied by a solitary customer, a plume-hatted leprechaun reading a newspaper. On the counter, behind speckled glass, is a tantalising display of pastries, biscuits and tarts. As you examine the display, the shop-keeper slips behind the counter and watches you, poker-faced, pinch-lipped and none too friendly.

You may buy something to eat if you have enough coins. Each selection has a three-digit reference which you must turn to if you wish to purchase the item. If you have some eye ointment and you would like to use it now, turn to 24. When you have finished making your purchases, turn to 5.

44

You try the key, but it does not work. You fumble for another key, glancing back to check the lane. To your horror, the winged shape of the Elemental is swooping low across the cobblestones. You are the prey, and this creature will be merciless. It is upon you within seconds. Deadly talons rip into your flesh. A triumphant shriek fills the air, accompanied by your final valiant cry as you slump to the ground, the smell of your own blood and death rising about you.

Turn to 332.

45

You utter the spell. To your relief, the vines recoil and become still. Shaking yourself from sleepiness, you run along the pathway until you come at last to another door.

Turn to 214.

46

At the back of the glasshouse, you notice a small door leading to an outside garden. You slip through the door, only to find the garden enclosed by a perilously high wall. There is nowhere to go. The sound of Pearlie's rasping laugh reaches your ears. Spooked, you dive under a bush of soft silver leaves, hoping the foliage will hide you.

You wait a while, heart beating furiously in your chest. At length you hear Hensoi hovering nearby in the garden.

'Ye can comme out, fer the scrobag be gone,' he calls.

You emerge from the bush, feeling a little sheepish. The herbalist frowns at the damage you've done to his plant.

'This be wyrmewoode,' he says, clearly upset.

You must appease the herbalist by giving him a copper coin. Make a note of your loss of geld, and turn to **139**.

47

'Then ye be of debt to me, halven-fey,' she says.

This does not sound like a good idea to you. You attempt to decline her offer, but you can see that Pearlie is no longer listening to you.

Make a note that you are indebted to Pearlie, and turn to **257**.

48

You step out into the lane. The goblins react with lightning speed, throwing themselves upon you like wild animals. The knife sinks into the thick fibre of your cloak, checked but nonetheless finding your flesh. A wave of pain washes over you as you collapse on the ground. You feel rough fingers searching your clothes, while your satchel is ripped from your grasp and the contents strewn across the lane. The goblins squabble over your precious possessions, then together they break into a run, arms and legs pin-wheeling down the lane. Their laughter echoes through the lanes until at last there is silence.

You stagger to your feet. A blood stain has soaked the upper part of your cloak. Still, you can walk, and you are greatly relieved to see that your spellbook was not stolen. The goblins, however, have taken all your money. You hastily pick up your remaining possessions and hobble over to the pigeon. The bird casts a glassy, terrified eye at you and takes off, lurching down the lane in short, desperate bursts of elevation. Remembering Pearlie's words, you hurry after it as best you can.

Make a note of your loss of geld and turn to **340**.

49

It is cool and dingy inside the shop and it smells strongly of sulphur and other medicines. Acrid candles burn atop the shelves beside glass jars and bottles of different coloured liquids. You cast your eye about the shop, at first not seeing anyone. Then you notice a cloaked figure at the back of the room. The figure unfurls from the shadows and shuffles into the candlelight, greeting you with a phlegmy cough. It is a tall faery, his willowy beard shimmering in the glow.

'Have ye an appointun?' he asks wheezily.

You shake your head and his gaze narrows.

'What be yer affair, then?' he asks.

Would you like to buy something (turn to **58**), or ask the doctor for advice (turn to **118**)?

50

You step outside the tavern into the busy street. A wintry sun fights its way down through bare branches and sagging rooftops, warming your face. You wrap your cloak around you and hoist your satchel on your shoulder.

Your attention is suddenly drawn to the sound of a ringing bell. *Ding! Ding! Ding-a-ling!* Glancing back down the street, you see an ornate contraption rumbling towards you. The smell of coal and metal fills the air. You step back and watch as a dilapidated machine on tram tracks approaches, puffs of steam trailing after it. It grinds to a halt before you. Round windows reveal the faces of passengers inside. A faery disembarks, spreading her wings as she steps onto the cobblestones.

Do you want to catch the tram (turn to **178**), or follow the tramline on foot (turn to **109**)?

51

You run as fast as you can, blood pounding through your veins. You know that if you meet the Elemental again you will almost certainly die. Exhausted and lost as you are, the turns of the lanes grow familiar. Your heart floods with relief as you come upon the lane by which you first entered, and at its end, the faithful church door.

Turn to **172**.

52

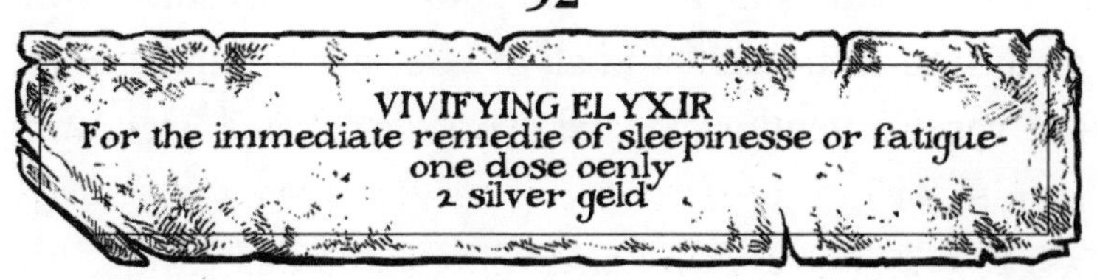

53

'Murn' you speak clearly at the door. A gust of wind blows up the steps as the door unlatches and swings slowly open. Lightning flashes in the sky. Drops of rain begin to fall. With relief, you at last enter the sanctuary of the Warlock's home.

Turn to **266**.

54

As you lean against the wall, a sudden and inexplicable cramp in your stomach causes you to cry out and double over in terrible pain.

'Theife!' you hear someone call.

Through glazed vision you see the merchant who sold you the quill pointing at you. Other passengers turn to look.

'The quill be charmed!' declares the merchant. 'It reveals a cross'd buyer, one who uses naught for geld!'

Triumphantly, the merchant holds up the small grey feather which you had enchanted with Cyleric's spell. You become aware of the glare of passengers watching, unsympathetic to the cramps which seize you.

There is only one way to rid yourself of this curse. You must return the quill and all of your other purchases to the various vendors. Make a note of your losses, and turn to **345**.

55

You find yourself crawling along a roughly-hewn passageway. The air is close and stale, the floor cold beneath your hands. Soon you are lost in pitch darkness, following only the sound of the creature's breathing as it leads you on. At last you see a square of greyish light ahead, and outside sounds penetrate your dulled senses: cars and people and the sounds of the city. You scramble towards your escape.

Turn to **112**.

56

You utter the spell as the bird swoops down on you. It veers suddenly and crashes into the stonework, landing on the cobblestones with a squawk and a tangle of flying feathers. The second bird circles in the sky, though it seems to sense your magic and you are relieved when at last it disappears.

You hurry back to the junction, stopping to count your coins. You have an extra six coppers and two gold coins.

Make a note of your new riches. You may now either follow the lane to the left (turn to **90**), or continue straight ahead (turn to **244**).

57

You carve your triangle roughly in the wood. Effie examines your move and carves a cross in reply. There is only one move you can make to stop her from getting three crosses in a row.

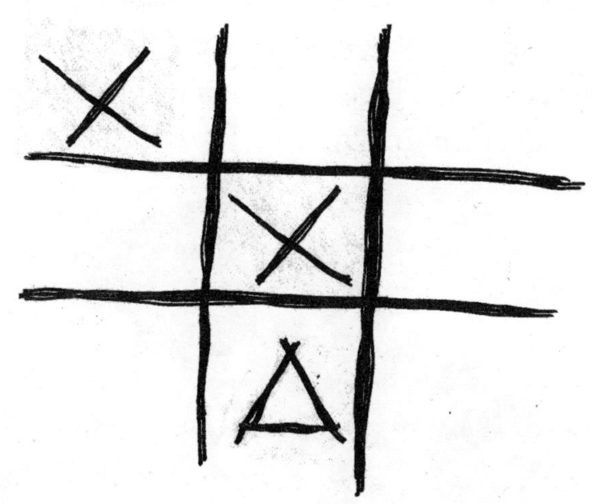

Turn to 184.

58

The doctor allows you to peruse the cabinets and shelves. The prices are all beyond your means, save for a collection of out-dated jars and bottles.

Make a note of this paragraph number, then turn to the numbers on the jars to read the labels. The cream and elixir each cost two silver coins. The eye ointment costs one gold coin. Buy as many as you like (or none at all), and then turn to 226.

59

You utter the spell. Before your eyes, the feathers are transformed into coins of copper. Cyleric laughs at your amazement.

'They be a goodlie guise. The best coin enchantment I have e'er seen, if I maye admit this myself. With a littel pracktise, ye will turn them to gold, if only for the time to buy a drinkun.'

You remember suddenly that you owe Cyleric a drink. Delighted with your new spell, you hurry to the bar.

Turn to **206**.

60

The door shuts behind you and you hear the tumblers lock. You shoulder your satchel and venture up the laneway to the main street. The snow has turned to a dirty slush on the cobblestones. The street is busy now with faeries and other strange folk going about their business, and you are pleased to see no sign of the oobanata. Even so, you are careful to keep hidden as a cart rolls by. A couple of pixies on the back spit at you as they pass. Friendly inhabitants of Suidemor, you think to yourself.

Safe for the moment in the shadows of the lane, you hunker down and open your spellbook, flicking through the brittle pages.

If you want to try a spell, you may do so now. You may try to either unlock a door or levitate an object. Add the number of the spell to this paragraph number and turn to the answer. If you would prefer to search for the Blackrose Arms, turn to **170**.

61

You utter the spell. The apparitions gawp at you, then one by one they pull away. Heart pounding, you step back into the doorway. With a quick glance to the ground rushing by below, you jump.

Turn to **34**.

62

You glance along the bar to see that a few fey are drinking a dark liquid from goblet-shaped glasses. It seems to be the house specialty. You point at the drink and ask for one. The barmaid remains expressionless as she serves you, requesting a payment of three copper coins for the drink.

You may pay her if you have the money (turn to 87), or decline the drink if you don't (turn to 137).

63

You utter the spell, but nothing happens. The bird dives at you, its beak tearing into the flesh of your shoulder. Pain sears through your arm.

These birds are magical. Your fear spell will only work on common fey. You must find another spell to ward off the birds, and quickly!

64

'Help!' you call out. The sound is feeble, deadened by the thick stone walls.

You will die if you stay here. You will have to try to climb the walls (turn to 29).

65

You turn into the lane: it is much the same as the last. An unnerving silence hangs in the air. You soon come across another junction.

Would you like to go right (turn to **90**) or continue on (turn to **171**)?

66

You sit up amid the buckets and flowers. The van has stopped deep in the tunnel. The driver turns to regard you with his unnerving and blood-shot eyes.

'We be safe here, for but a moment,' he tell you in a sandpapery voice. 'Them birds cannot abide the scent of the magical flowers.'

He glances ruefully at the flowers and buckets strewn in the van. Though he speaks in English, you wonder at his strange accent.

'I be a greeper, good with hands and dirt, and a loyal servant of the Elder Oeda. She be the goodlie sister of the King Othirom, and she has sent ye this.'

He holds out a grubby-looking satchel with his mud-caked hand. You take the satchel.

'Open it,' the greeper impresses.

Wordlessly, you do as he asks. Inside you find a small leather-bound book. The cover and spine are blank, as are the pages. Inside is an envelope, also blank. As you inspect it, however, a fine gold script appears, addressed to you:

Anivad, born of Eleonore

You hastily open the envelope. Inside is a similiarly blank piece of parchment, though as you stare at it, the words begin to appear:

Dearen Anivad,
Ye be in mæst danger, for ye have escapenned the tower of Olcrada, brother of the King of the Elder FeY. For this he wyll seek his revenge and murder ye at next chancE. Ye must do as I say if ye want to survive but one nyght in Suidemor. Seeketh ye the one who knoweth the Forgotten Spell...

Before you can finish reading, you are startled by the sound of an eerie wind whistling through the tunnel. Without further warning, the parchment is torn from your hands by a gust so strong that the van itself is buffeted from side to side.

'Oobanata!' whispers the greeper.

He starts the engine and the van splutters to life. With a crunch of gears and a belch of smoke, the van takes off, barrelling towards the exit. Before you can ask what the 'oobanata' might be, the van is picked up by the force of the wind like a toy car and shunted into the daylight. In a swirl of leaf litter and icy air, it is blown clear across a courtyard and slammed into a wall. You are thrown from the back as the vehicle crashes. You land hard on the cobblestone ground, and for a moment you can do nothing but watch, stunned, as the vehicle explodes into flame.

Turn to **101**.

67

After your long night's work, you feel extraordinarily tired. You limp into the cluttered back room to find Garda standing at the pot-bellied stove, stirring gruel in a saucepan and attending to a kettle of boiling water.

You drop the books on the ground, exhausted. Garda eyes you suspiciously.

'Wot be the matter with ye? Be ye cursed?' she asks.

She grabs hold of your arm roughly, exposing the marks where the nettles have stung you. You flinch from the pain, which seems to have only got worse.

'Witchy nettles – they be deadly plants, indeed,' she mutters. 'I can do naught to help ye. Ye must find a remedie soon by the ken of a doktor.'

She turns, leaving you to sink into a nearby armchair. A few moments later, she brings you a steaming bowl of some thick and lumpy substance and a cup of strong-smelling tea. You accept the food gratefully.

Garda reaches down for the pile of books, then pauses, staring at the books in utter amazement.

'Ye did finden it,' she whispers, picking up the third and smallest book – a thin volume bound in frayed blue cloth. 'This booke be blank … the writings be nun read by common fey, nun the insides nore the outsides. If ye did finden it, then there be but one answer to the riddle: ye have the Elder Fey sight – indeed, ye be Elder Fey.'

Garda stares at you, somewhat in awe. You remember the strange blank book in your satchel, and the message on the parchment that was blown from your hands.

Will you show Garda the book (turn to **99**) or hide your knowledge (turn to **88**)?

68

You utter the spell as the apparitions press against your body. These creatures are spirits, and your spell only works on material beings. Both of your wrists are now bound. With horror, you sense the pale fingers curling around your neck. You gasp for breath, beating helplessly at the creatures. Your final breath is a silent scream, as blackness envelops you.

Turn to **368**.

69

You explain hastily that you haven't enough money. The barmaid glares at you, snatching the drinks off the table and stalking away. The dwarf turns to you angrily.

'Blacken the name of mine table!' he sneers, grabbing your arm. His calloused dwarf fingers dig painfully into your skin.

Will you try and cast a spell, or wrest yourself free (turn to 38)?

70

You carefully examine the walls. There are several stones which are untouched by nettles and may provide you safe purchase. But where will you climb to? You stare at the grated window high above, wondering if you will die in this terrible place, and thinking with horror about the fate that may have befallen your mother.

Then you notice something odd – that bits of powdery dirt are falling from the cracks around a large stone right above you. A scraping sound reaches your ears. The stone begins to loosen and is pushed further and further out. You gather your senses to jump aside, as the stone leans precariously for a moment, then crashes to the floor. There is a tremendous cracking sound as the stone splinters the floorboards. The dust settles into silence, and you look up to see a neat rectangular hole.

To reach the hole, you must climb the wall without touching the nettles. Examine the picture opposite. You will see that certain stones on the facing wall have no nettles growing on them – these are safe stones. To solve the puzzle, count the number of safe stones in the picture and turn to the answer. If you cannot solve the puzzle, turn to 131 before you use the Puzzle Solver.

71

You mutter the spell. The merchant looks at you in fright, rather like he's seen a ghost. He gathers up his candles and retreats quickly into the crowd. You notice several passengers turn to stare at you, fearful and whispering. It seems like a good time to disembark. You hastily pull the bell. Gears grind underfoot as the tram slows. A breath of cold air greets you as you step down from the tram.

Turn to 222.

72

You sit on the damp floor, fighting your growing panic. There is a dead silence all about you. Minutes pass, becoming hours. No one comes for you. Nothing happens.

You will die if you stay here. You will have to try to climb the walls. Turn to 29.

73

You duck into the alleyway. It is extremely narrow and littered with junk. You pick your way between pieces of broken furniture and smashed crockery. All is quiet and yet you sense someone watching. You glance upwards, scanning the pale sliver of sky between the buildings. Windows sulk behind bits of board. A string of wet laundry drips between rusty balustrades.

The stillness is broken by a voice from high above.

'Goe away!' calls the voice.

As you watch, something is thrown from an upper window – a heavy object which plummets straight towards you! You dive to safety, throwing yourself under the overhang of a disused doorway as the heavy object crashes to the ground. Shards of pottery fly through the air. Onions and potatoes bounce across the cobblestones.

'Goe away!' rants the voice again.

This time a collection of bottles comes hurtling towards you. The bottles smash against the stonework, creating a shower of lethal glass. You cry out as a piece lodges in your arm. Without delay, you run from the alleyway.

Turn to **116**.

74

You utter the spell as the apparitions press against your body. These creatures are spirits, and the magic that enchants them is far too strong to undo with an elementary spell. Both of your wrists are now bound. With horror, you sense the pale fingers curling around your neck. You gasp for breath, beating helplessly at the creatures. Your final breath is a silent scream, as blackness envelops you.

Turn to **368**.

75

Triumphant, you carve the triangle and slash a line through the winning row. Effie gawps at you, then uses both fists to plunge her knife into the table.

'Effie's table,' she says. The knife glints menacingly.

Turn to 223.

76

The door is latched behind you, locking in an odour of second-hand books and old slippers. Shelves of books are illuminated by lamplight. The old woman mutters some magic at the door.

'Ye'll be needings food and rest,' she says, cocking a dark and beady eye at you, 'and I'll be needing payement for my givings.'

Garda turns on her heel and leads you to the back of the cluttered shop. A curtain opens into a room with old furnishings. Books are piled on every surface. Wood burns in a stove, warming the cluttered space. Although you would like to stay by the fire, Garda grabs you by the shirt and ushers you down a short corridor to another door. With her papery hands she searches through a bunch of keys.

'I be needing some help, as it happens,' she murmurs, as she unlocks the door.

Turn to 113.

77

As Garda Grye predicted, the nettle poison is taking its toll. You feel weak and your skin is pale and clammy. As you approach the shop, the faery stops sweeping the snow and looks at you in alarm.

'Doktor!' he cries, waving you down the street. He clearly doesn't want you in his shop.

You stumble along the pavement in the direction of his waving, soon arriving at a window filled with bottles and jars. A makeshift repair hides a crack in the glass, partly obscuring the words:

MedicinarY
For assessment of ailments
and administration of medicinneS
~CLOSED~

You knock urgently on the shop door.

Turn to 249.

78

You search your satchel and pockets for something to give.

You may offer any one of your remaining possessions, including coins. Make a note of your loss and turn to **36**. If you have nothing to give, you must be on your way (turn to 222).

79

Hensoi wipes his hands on his apron and flies into the shop to greet his customer. You linger in the glasshouse, hesitant to follow him.

Will you follow Hensoi and leave through the front door (turn to 209), or look for an escape out the back of the shop (turn to 46)?

80

You take the compass out and peer into the glass. The needle quivers, indicating that you should turn right. You walk up the lane, your footsteps crunching on dead leaves and fallen twigs. You soon come across another junction. You follow the compass needle to the right again. The path is claustrophobically narrow and thick with brambles. You proceed slowly, picking your way around the bare branches until the path begins to slope downwards, eventually coming to a tunnel, overgrown and choked with dead brambles.

It is going to be dangerous navigating the tunnel in the dark. Do you have a candle? If you do, turn to 292. If not, turn to 141.

TRAMME SERVYCES

Servyce	Schedule	Carriage
9	most dayes	Mail tramme
16	everie other daye	Market tramme
17	everie full moon	Witche's tramme
22	some dayes	Common tramme
3	now and again	Trolle tramme
13	4 O'Clock	Unseelie tramme
12	nyght~time	Goodes tramme
27	twilight	Ghoules tramme

For more accurate times, please asken of Time~Keeper

81

As you step back into the street, you are accosted by the smell of coal and metal and the sound of ringing bells. *Ding! Ding! Ding-a-ling!* A dilapidated contraption on tram tracks has come to a stop in the middle of the road. You watch as a faerie disembarks, spreading her wings. The bells ring again and the tram heaves forward along the tracks, puffs of soot and steam trailing after it.

Cyleric had said to follow the tramline. Beside the road is a signpost with what looks to be a timetable pinned to it. You stop to examine it, finding a grime-stained parchment that indicates the various services of the tram route. As you stand there, a little door hidden in the grain of the wood flies open. The door is only inches high, as is the little fey who stands in the doorway glaring at you. Her round belly is covered by a fat-splattered apron and in one hand she brandishes a tiny mixing spoon. She waves it at you and yells.

'Nun more tramme times! The castle forgetten to paye us. Nun paye, nun times!' She beats her spoon on the doorframe, then adds, a shrewdness in her eye, 'We do take charities, how-the-ever.'

Do you want to pay the time-keeper for more information? If so, you may use either a real coin or your remaining enchanted copper (turn to **37**). If you do not wish to pay the time-keeper, you can thank her and be on your way (turn to **109**).

82

You grab hold of the grilles and hoist yourself into the back of the van. It takes off suddenly, reversing out of the alley and toppling the flower buckets. Water and flowers spray through the air as the van swerves into the street. Hanging onto the grille, you glance up at the building from which you escaped. Clutches of crows sit huddled on the ivy-choked window ledges. One of them calls ominously. These are not ordinary birds; they are guardians of the tower. The black shapes suddenly take flight, heading straight towards the van in a dive-bombing formation that does not look friendly! You throw yourself upon the floor of the van.

Turn to **169**.

83

The door opens upon a narrow lane. Cold air stings your face as you step outside. The door shuts behind you. Looking back, you see that it appears to be quite ordinary from the outside, its wooden panels roughened with age and beaten by weather. You try the handle and find that it is now locked.

The lane is utterly deserted. The stone walls are covered in a thick hedge of thorny branches. High above, thunderous clouds gather in the sky, heavy with rain. Night is coming, and with it will come the brewing storm and unknown dangers. You hope to find the Warlock sooner than be caught in the dark.

You begin walking, your boots crunching on the hedge litter. The lane is straight and narrow, and, apart from the rose hedge, seemingly featureless. An eerie silence surrounds you. Shortly you come to another lane, identical in appearance, leading away to your right.

If you have a compass, turn to **20**. Otherwise, you may turn right (turn to **318**), or continue on (turn to **331**).

84

You mutter the spell. Immediately, the merchant's candles begin to float out of his pockets and up to the ceiling! The merchant curses you and chases quickly after them, standing on chairs and other passengers to gather them up. Several fey turn to look at you, annoyed. It seems like a good time to disembark. You hastily pull the bell. Tram gears grind underfoot as the tram slows. A breath of cold air greets you as you step down onto the pavement.

Turn to 222.

85

You approach a shop window dressed with bottles and jars. A makeshift repair hides a crack in the glass, partly obscuring the words:

MedicinarY
For assessment of ailments
and administration of medicinneS
~OPEN~

You push the shop door.

Turn to 49.

86

You sidestep the mess and are about to continue on your way when you hear a low growling sound from a doorway on your left. Whatever is behind the door has heard you – or smelt you. Heart racing, you take another step. To your horror, the door swings open and exposes a mangy animal, half dog, half wolf, standing over a stash of bloodied meat, its maddened eyes gleaming. The creature growls as it drops a piece of fetid flesh and takes a step towards you.

You will have to cast a spell immediately!

87

You pay for the drink. Expensive as it is, it smells good. You take a sip. To your surprise, the drink tastes beautiful. Comforted by the warmth and sweetness, you quickly finish it.

As you place the glass on the bar, your head feels suddenly foggy. You realise that this faery potion is very alcoholic. The sounds of the tavern merge into a single throbbing noise that fills your head. Colour seems to drain from the world. You clutch at the bar to steady yourself, but your fingers slip off the wood as you fall to the floor.

If you have a bottle of vivifying elixir, turn to 95. If not, turn to 22.

88

You tell Garda that you have never heard of the Elder Fey. She glowers at you.

'Do nun try to pull the wool o'er Garda's sharpe eyes! Suche writings be impossible to see unless ye be of the Elder Fey. I care naught what blood ye be, for I will surely turn ye to Olcrada if there be scent of deceit about ye.'

Garda sets her mouth grimly. There is little doubt that she will carry out her threat if needed, and that you need all the help you can get.

Turn to **99**.

89

You step from the shadows and command the goblins to release the bird. They gape at you, caught off guard. One of them spits on the ground. You advance as menacingly as you can. They retreat, both breaking into a run, their arms and legs pin-wheeling down the laneway.

You will have to chase the goblins.

Turn to **150**.

90

You enter the lane. It is claustrophobically narrow and thick with brambles. You proceed slowly, picking your way around the bare branches. The path begins to slope downwards, eventually coming to a tunnel, overgrown and choked with dead brambles.

Navigating the tunnel in the dark will be dangerous. Do you have a candle? If you do, turn to 292. If not, turn to 141.

91

You carve your triangle roughly in the wood. Effie examines your move and carves a cross in reply. There is only one move you can make to stop her from getting three crosses in a row

Turn to 144.

92

You accept the drink. The faery slams his coins enthusiastically on the bar top.

'Two o' the best drinks!' he tells the barmaid.

She replies sharply that he can only afford the worst. You watch as she pours a dark liquid into two goblet-shaped glasses. The faery grins and picks up a glass.

'Pucker be one o' me næmes,' he tells you.

You can smell the drink on his breath as he hands you your glass. The liquid is warm and smells spicy and good. You take a sip. To your surprise, the drink tastes wonderful.

'It be the wine for all sorrows,' he says, grinning as you quickly finish it.

As you place the glass on the bar, your head feels suddenly foggy. You realise that this faery potion is very alcoholic. The sounds of the tavern merge into a single throbbing noise that fills your head. You see Pucker speaking to you, but you cannot hear the words. Colour seems to drain from the world. You clutch at the bar to steady yourself, but your fingers slip off the wood as you fall to the floor.

If you have a bottle of vivifying elixir, turn to **4**. If not, turn to **22**.

93

Garda is already leading you from the shop as you ask her about the Forgotten Spell. She grows angry.

'Pah! What do I ken of fancie spels? They be fer the likes of Elder Fey who think themselves grand!'

It is clear she has no information for you. You mutter your thanks as she unlocks the door.

'Ye came in the back entrance, though ye best take the front entrance to leave.' She mumbles some magic at the lock and turns the latch. The door opens.

Turn to **100**.

94

You utter the spell as the second bird swoops down on you. It veers suddenly and crashes into the stonework, landing on the cobblestones with a squawk and a tangle of flying feathers.

Gritting your teeth against the pain in your arm, you hobble back to the junction. Nightfall is approaching, and with a wound to tend, your progress will be slowed. You must find your way to the Arch Warlock as fast as you can.

Make a note that you have been injured by the magpies, and also that you have an extra six coppers and two gold coins. You may now either follow the lane to the left (turn to **90**), or continue straight ahead (turn to **244**).

95

You fumble in your satchel for the vivifying elixir. You quickly unstopper the bottle and take a sip of the liquid. Your body is wracked by a chill. When you open your eyes, you see the faces of faeries gathered around you, laughing and pointing at your dilemma.

'Can nun hold the spirut!' cries one.

You pull yourself quickly to your feet. You glance around for support, but there is none. It seems to be time to take your leave.

Turn to **186**.

You dash across the road, taking your life into your hands as vehicles swerve to miss you. Reaching the pavement safely, you spy the narrow alleyway into which the creature disappeared. Parked there in the gloom is an open-topped van filled to the brim with buckets of colourful flowers. The creature awaits you, seated behind the wheel with his face hidden by the cowl of his cloak.

Will you climb aboard (turn to **82**) or ask questions first (turn to **135**)?

97

Relief floods over you as you stumble forward, not into the jaws of the Elemental, but into a wide and gracious corridor. You stand, shaken by your brush with death and awed by the sight before you. The corridor is filled with the light of a thousand small, flickering lanterns that dance overhead. You gawp in amazement, realising that the lights are not lanterns at all – they are faeries, each one smaller than the palm of your hand. Like shy, luminous moths, they flutter away from you. Arches of white stone adorn the ceiling for as far as the eye can see.

A gleaming floor invites you into the sanctuary of what can only be a library, for the corridor is lined with shelves of ivory-spined books. You step forward into the cool, stale air, safe for the moment from Olcrada's pursuit, following the destiny that beckons ahead.

Turn to **370**.

98

You utter the spell, but nothing happens. The bird dives at you, its beak tearing into the flesh of your shoulder. Pain sears through your arm.

These birds are magical. Your slumber spell will only work on common fey. You must find another spell to ward off the birds, and quickly!

99

You pull the book from your satchel. For a moment the cover is blank, but as you stare at it, you begin to perceive a fine writing embossed across the worn cover.

The Orughadh of the Elder Fey

'What say it?' asks Garda.

You read it aloud to her as best you can.

'The Ordughadh!' she snorts. 'The magic royaltie, they fashion themselves.'

She snatches the book and flicks the pages.

'It be invisiblie to my common eyes. Ye have the Elder Fey sight, though it be strange enough, fer ye be liken as Mortal, with Mortal blood. Perhappen ye be halven-fey, half of eache, though I have ne'er seen suche a being before. I have heard only tell of their power, and of their blackened luck.'

She glares at you.

'Where am I?' you ask, your head reeling.

'Suidemor, halven. The city of Faery,' replies Garda. She tosses the book back at you. You save it from landing in the half-eaten bowl of gruel.

The city of Faery.... You have been brought here by Olcrada, but for what purpose, you do not know. Your life is in danger, and whoever sent you this book is trying to protect you. You open the book to the first page. At first the page is blank, but the words soon appear, written in fine ink:

The Eight Spells of Elementary Elder Magic

A spellbook! You turn the pages excitedly.

You will find the spellbook at the back of this book. You may take it with you and refer to it whenever you like. Each spell is numbered. If you are given the option to cast a spell, you must add the number of the spell to the number of the paragraph you are on. If the spell has been cast, the paragraph you turn to will be marked with this symbol:

If there is no symbol, then you will have to try another spell or choose a different option. Your ability to cast spells depends on your level of experience and sometimes on your circumstances. Sometimes your spell will have no effect, but you will still see the symbol, in which case you must read on.

Take time to look through the spellbook now. When you are finished, turn to **219**.

100

You step outside. The alleyway by which you entered is now gone, and in its place is a wide street lined with dilapidated shops, bathed in early morning sunshine and a light covering of snow. All is quiet. Across the road a faery sweeps the snow from outside his door. His wings glisten in the sunshine as he works. Behind him, stained awnings hang like sleepy eyelids, obscuring the windows. You glance down the street. A bell tinkles as a motorised contraption approaches in the distance, putt-putting and clanking, loaded up with bottles of milk. Still further away are the sounds of doors opening and closing and water pipes groaning. All seems peaceful, but as you stand in the shadow of the bookshop door, you feel the gaze of unfriendly eyes. You are being hunted. A gust of wind chills your face as you try to recall the message from the Elder Oeda:

... Seeketh ye the one who knoweth
the Forgotten Spell ...

Your stomach knots in fear; there are forces which did not want you to see the rest of that message. You must leave this conspicuous doorway of Garda Grye's shop before you are found. But where should you go?

You may find shelter in the alleyway (turn to 73), seek refuge in the shop across the road (turn to **189**) or ask the milkman for help (turn to **176**).

101

The sharp smell of petrol and flames fills the air. Smoke billows from the crashed van, and through dazed vision you see a flock of crows scattering high above. You can see no sign of the greeper.

Will you check the burning vehicle (turn to **6**) or flee the scene immediately (turn to **147**)?

102

You decline Hensoi's offer. Just then you hear the shop bell tinkling. The miniature trees shiver in a draught of cold air, and a pungent smell reaches your nose. Hensoi peers into the shop.

'Who be in my shoppe?' he calls out nervously.

You see a hunched figure dressed in rags standing near the doorway.

''Tis oenly Pearlie, little fey, in need of some goodlie herbes,' a rasping voice replies.

Have you seen Pearlie in another shop? If so, turn to **120**. If not, turn to **79**.

103

The tram rumbles forward, gathering speed. The passengers seem curious about you. They begin to leave their seats one by one, gathering around you with ghostly arms outstretched. One of them strokes the fabric of your cloak. You beat off the hand, only to find the long pale fingers curling around your wrist. Do you have any ghoul's thistle? If so, turn to **166**. If not, turn to **133**.

104

You carve your triangle roughly in the wood. Effie examines your move and carves a cross in reply. There is only one move you can make to stop her from getting three crosses in a row.

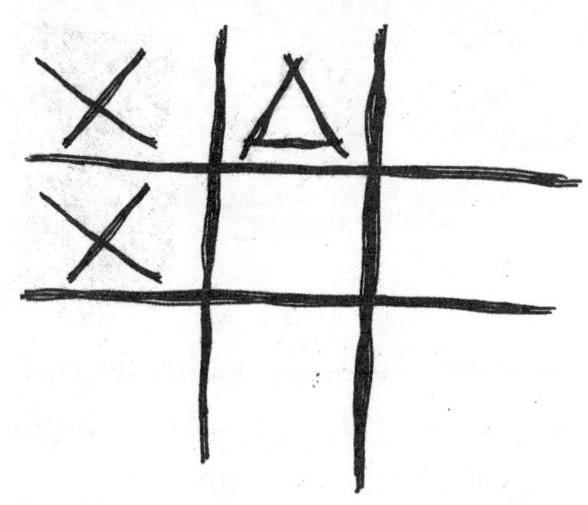

Turn to 311.

105

'Help!' you call out. The sound is feeble, deadened by the thick stone walls.

Will you try to climb the walls (turn to 29), or sit tight and see if someone comes for you (turn to 72)?

106

You mutter the spell. The merchant's eyes become glazed and his eyelids heavy. His shoulders droop and he slumps to the floor with a thud. Several passengers turn to stare at the sleeping merchant. It seems like a good time to disembark. You hastily pull the bell. Tram gears grind underfoot as the tram slows. A breath of cold air greets you as you step down onto the pavement.

Turn to 222.

107

You mutter the spell. A flicker of doubt crosses the dwarf's features, but his grip remains strong.

You will have to wrest yourself free (turn to 38).

108

You reach into your satchel and find the precious jar. You drink the liquid as fast as you can, willing your throat to swallow even as your breath constricts in the deadly air. A warm sensation fills your body. Your muscles twitch and quiver in readiness, your legs feel solid beneath you. You turn and run.

Make a note that you have used up the vivifying elixir, and turn to 163.

109

Following the tramline, you continue along the pavement of cobblestones, hoping to blend in with the pedestrians. You walk under the faded awnings, passing shop windows displaying strange wares. Vendors vie for your custom, but you keep your business to yourself and your eyes averted from their shrewd stares.

Gradually the shops diminish and are replaced with boarded-up doorways and broken windows. You pass a few faeries. They keep their heads down, hurrying to their unimaginable destinations as the city darkens under a gauze of grey cloud.

Under the shelter of an eave, you pause to tighten your cloak about your shoulders. You are about to continue on your way when you hear a moaning coming from the doorway. You glance down to see a pale, groping hand emerging from what appears to be a bundle of rags on the ground. The hand, you notice, is missing three fingers.

'Charitie!' breathes a miserable voice from beneath the rags.

Will you offer the creature something (turn to 78), or quickly be on your way (turn to 222)?

110

You ask the dwarf how his meal fares. He looks up from his plate, grease dribbling down his chin, and appraises your appearance with bulbous, bloodshot eyes.

'What be yer affair?' he grunts.

Will you now ask him about the Forgotten Spell (turn to **247**), or offer to buy him a drink in exchange for a seat at his table (turn to **23**)?

111

You focus on the spellbook and utter the spell. To your amazement, the book lurches upwards just inches from your hands. It hiccups in the air, wobbles on its side, then crashes to the ground and lands in a puddle of snow slush.

Perhaps you just need some practice. You retrieve your sodden book and prepare to try the spell again. Just then, you hear the sounds of running feet and shouting. You quickly press yourself into the shadows of the lane.

Turn to **200**.

112

You emerge into a damp and drizzly daylight. You are standing at the mouth of a drainway, set in the outer wall of a towering building of stone and steel. Enormous buttresses cast a menacing shadow over the scene before you: a streetscape of the strangest buildings you have ever seen, all crammed together at odd angles, facing a busy road that you do not recognise. Vehicles whizz past at reckless speeds, belching steam and smoke into the air, while others are powered by galloping horses.

The smell of manure mingles with soot and the sounds of engines and hooves. You hug the precariously narrow pavement in alarm as a bicycle-like contraption hurtles past. The cyclist is a faery, only three feet high! Billowing behind her, like sails, is a pair of translucent wings.

You try to quell your rising sense of panic. You are sure of only one thing – this is not your city! You catch sight of the creature who has aided you, waiting for you on the other side of the street. You see that he is half your stature and covered by a cloak. Then he disappears between the buildings. You hasten to follow.

Turn to **96**.

113

The door creaks open. Broken cobwebs fall down to greet you and the room exhales a gust of musty air. The one window you can see is trapped by a thick layer of books and broken furniture.

'Ye are to finden three bookes,' Garda says.

She pulls out a scrap of parchment from her shapeless dress. On the paper are drawn three symbols:

You take the piece of parchment from Garda. She glares at you, not quite trusting you to do the job. Then she pockets her keys and without a word turns and leaves, closing the door behind her. You gaze up at the junk. There are hundreds of books, and they are all coded in symbols.

Take your time to find the right books. Each symbol has a number next to it. When you have found the books, put the numbers together in the order on the parchment and turn to that number.

114

You fumble in your satchel for the vivifying elixir. You quickly unstopper the bottle and take a sip of the liquid. Your body is wracked by a chill. When you open your eyes, you see the dwarf and several onlookers standing over you and laughing.

'Can nun hold his spirut!' cries one.

You pull yourself to your feet.

'Next time ye will mind yer plæce, feyling,' sneers the dwarf.

With as much dignity as you can muster, you slip into the crowd, ignoring the jeers behind you.

Turn to **186**.

115

You carve your triangle roughly in the wood. Effie examines your move and carves a cross in reply. There is only one move you can make to stop her from getting three crosses in a row.

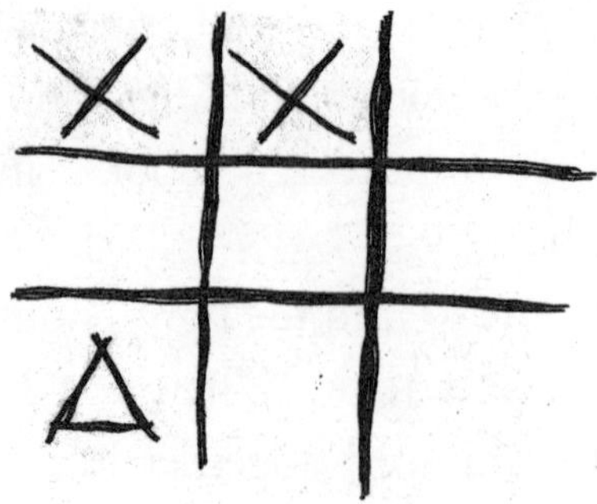

Turn to **190**.

116

You glance up and down the street frantically. You are bleeding and you must find help. You stagger across the road to the cluster of sleepy shops. Many of them are boarded up and dark within. You pass the grimy windows of a bakery and the eerie glow of a green-tinted glass door proclaiming the services of a herbalist. Further down the street you find a window dressed with bottles and jars. A makeshift repair hides a crack in the glass, partly obscuring the words:

MedicinarY

For assessment of ailments
and administration of medicinneS

~ CLOSED ~

You knock urgently on the shop door.

Turn to 249.

117

You agree to Cyleric's terms. He exhales deeply, rubbing his forehead. When he draws another breath, you see that he has lost all trace of drunkenness, and that his eyes are clear and his presence has grown powerful. The fine skin of his wings shimmers with life. When he speaks, his voice is soft.

'There are alle kinds of magick in the world. There be the magick of the spiruts and ghouls, magick of dwarves and even trolls, and magick of the witches, called Witcherie. But nun be so powerful as the magick of the Elder Fey, fer it be the magick of number. Numbers be found everywhere and in everything – if you knoweth how to see them.'

Cyleric clears the space on the table between you.

'Before ye see the numbers, you must be trained to *see*. To see by the eyes of an Elder Fey, for by these eyes everything in the world can be chænged into the unspoken word of number. Wunce ye have begunne to see the world as suche, ye will beginne to unlock the power of these numbers and to change them for your own devyce. This be called Elder Magic.'

Cyleric falls silent. His eyes flash as he pulls the knife from the folds of his cloak. The blade flickers as he deftly scores a line in the wood of the table. You watch as a shape emerges beneath the blade. Carved there is a perfect pentagon, inside which a series of interconnected lines form an arrangement of triangles.

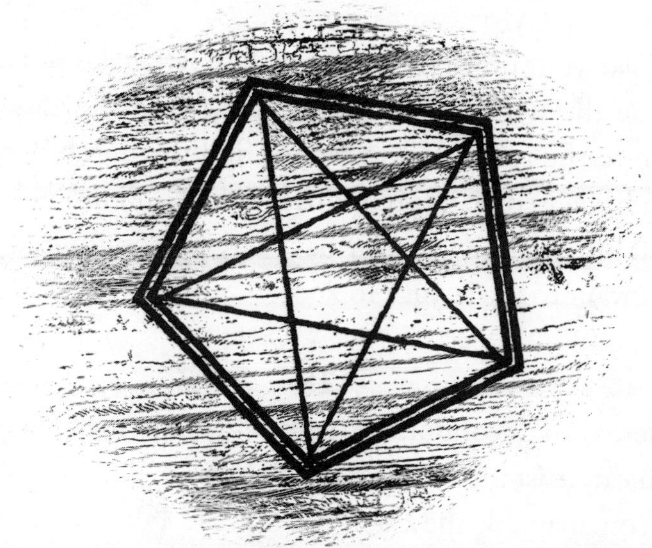

Cyleric retires the knife to his cloak and speaks from the shadows.

'This be an ancient glyph of Elder Magic,' he tells you reverently. 'It be filled wyth numbers, some hidden, some not. Ye must finden the number called the *First Hidden*. It be the number of triangles which ye can see by your eyes.'

You gaze at the symbol carved in the wood.

'It maye first seem simpelie, but your first guessen wyll be certain wrong. Be timely and caringful. Only when your mind has unlocked the truest answer will ye awaken your abilitie to see the world in number and to pracktise your magick. But take heed, I can nun help ye. Ye must see the answer for yeself, or else be suffered in your arte,' Cyleric warns you.

Take your time now to count all the triangles you can see in the symbol. When you have found the answer, turn to the result. If you cannot find the number, and you have used up all your Puzzle Solver options, turn to **361**. Alternatively, if you have any eye ointment and you want to use it, turn to **253**.

118

There is an uncomfortable pause as you decide how well you can trust the doctor, and what to ask him.

You may ask the doctor about the Forgotten Spell (turn to **18**). Alternatively, if Garda gave you a book to deliver to the Arch Warlock, you may add the number on the front of the book to this number and turn to the answer. Or, if you prefer, you may buy something instead (turn to **58**).

119

You politely refuse the drink. The faery scowls.

'Not goodlie enough fer the likes of ye?' he chides.

The barmaid waves him on with a look of disgust.

'Go and collect the slops insteaed of buthering fey!' she says.

The faery feigns hurt at her words and staggers off. You thank the barmaid, but she only grimaces at you and asks for your custom.

Will you buy a drink (turn to **62**), or ask her if she knows of the Forgotten Spell (turn to **221**)?

120

Hensoi wipes his hands on his apron and flies into the shop to greet his customer. You follow him, head bowed and muttering your thanks as you quickly duck through the shop. You feel Pearlie watching you. A short but terrible laugh escapes her lips. As you reach the safety of the open doorway, she catches your wrist with her icy hand.

''Tis only Pearlie!' she rasps at you.

Turn to **148**.

121

You carve your triangle. Effie expels a breathy grunt as she examines your move. She carves her next cross. You see immediately that she has made a big mistake. There is only one move you need to make to win three triangles in a row.

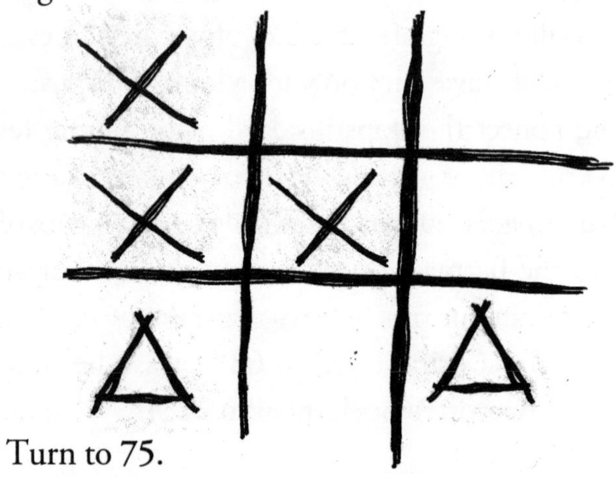

Turn to 75.

122

As Garda Grye predicted, the nettle poison is taking its toll, for you feel weak and your skin is clammy. You cross the road, passing the grimy windows of a bakery and the eerie glow of a green-tinted glass door proclaiming the services of a herbalist. Further down the street you find a window dressed with bottles and jars. A makeshift repair hides a crack in the glass, partly obscuring the words:

MedicinarY
For assessment of ailments
and administration of medicinneS
CLOSED

You knock urgently on the shop door.

Turn to **249**.

123

Hoping you have the correct order for the bowls, you sup from the ones you think you need. The Warlock watches you grimly. Your attempt to guess was as brave as it was doomed. You feel a sudden stab of pain in your stomach. You cry out, doubling over on the mossy floor as the pain stabs again.

'Fool ye nun with the powers of Witcherie,' intones the Arch Warlock, 'fer death be the penance.'

Sure enough, as the pain wracks your body, your vision fails and you fall into darkness…

Turn to **368**.

124

You utter the spell as the animal strikes. You are knocked to the ground, but the beast retreats immediately, whimpering and sniffing at the cold air. It backs into the doorway from which it came, keeping its eyes on you until it disappears into the shadows.

You stagger to your feet. Pain flares in your shoulder. You glance down to see the torn fabric of your cloak and blood running down your arm. Nursing the wound, you hobble down the lane to safety.

Make a note that you have been injured by the dog, and turn to **230**.

125

You heave yourself up, pulling your full weight onto the stone. The nettles lash at you like whips. You cry out, jumping back to the ground as pain sears through your arm. There is a raw, red mark on your skin.

The nettles are not only painful, they are also poisonous. Make a note that you have been stung by the nettles, and turn to **70**.

126

You hurry back to Pearlie's door and stand before it. You utter the spell, but nothing happens. You turn the doorknob and it comes off in your hand. It seems you have broken the door instead of unlocking it!

Perhaps you just need some practice. You push the doorknob back in place and prepare to try the spell again. Just then, you hear the sounds of running feet and shouting. You quickly press yourself into the shadows of the lane.

Turn to **200**.

127

You wait, still and hardly breathing. The knife blades flash menacingly as the goblins survey their surroundings. They retreat slowly, then break together into a run, arms and legs pin-wheeling down the laneway.

You will have to chase the goblins. Turn to **150**.

128

You wrench yourself free of her grasp and dash into the street.

'Halven-fey!' cries Pearlie, shuffling after you.

You could easily outrun her, but something draws you to a stop. You glance about, noticing that the street is deathly silent but for the sound of the shop door slamming behind you. A thickness invades the air, something foreign and searching, something which fills you with a dread far worse than the breath of the hag who pursues you. Staring into the street, you see tendrils of vapour, the colour of deep bruises, slithering along the cobblestones like snakes, creeping up walls and into windows, sliding under doors and coiling themselves around lamp-posts. Pearlie wails and you turn to see her running down the street, her rags flapping behind her.

Do you have the strength to follow Pearlie? If you were stung by the nettles (even if you were cured) turn to **267**. If you were not, turn to **163**.

129

You utter the spell as the second bird swoops down on you. It veers suddenly and crashes into the stonework, landing on the cobblestones with a squawk and a tangle of flying feathers.

Gritting your teeth against the pain in your arm, you hobble back to the junction. Nightfall is approaching, and with a wound to tend, your progress will be slowed. You must find your way to the Arch Warlock as fast as you can.

Make a note that you have been injured by the magpies, and also that you have an extra six coppers and two gold coins. You may now either follow the lane to the left (turn to **90**), or continue straight ahead (turn to **244**).

130

You bravely pull out the little knife and prepare to face the Elemental. The creature advances and your grip on the knife tightens. As it lunges forward, you strike, sinking the knife into the taut muscle of its body. A shriek fills the air and the creature lashes out. Its talons slice across your shoulder and you feel a searing pain. With your knife now lost, you run, terrified, back down the lane.

Make a note that you have been struck by an Air Elemental and turn to 51.

131

You step on the wrong stone and a nettle lashes at you. You drop to the ground, crying out in pain. The nettle leaves a red mark on your skin.

Make a note that you have been stung by the nettles. You may now turn to the Puzzle Solver to find the answer.

132

Hoping you have the correct order for the bowls, you sup from the ones you think you need. The Warlock watches you grimly. Your attempt to guess was as brave as it was doomed. You feel a sudden stab of pain in your stomach. You cry out, doubling over on the mossy floor as the pain stabs again.

'Fool ye nun with the powers of Witcherie,' intones the Arch Warlock, 'fer death be the penance.'

Sure enough, as the pain wracks your body, your vision fails and you fall into darkness...

Turn to **368**.

133

Panicked, you fumble for the door but the apparitions surround you, jamming you against the wall. Both of your wrists are bound by their grasp. With horror, you sense the pale fingers curling around your neck. You gasp for breath, beating helplessly at the creatures. Your final breath is a silent scream. Blackness envelops you.

Turn to **368**.

134

This bun smells so delicious that you cannot help but eat it on the spot. However, it is so very sweet and very sticky that you immediately feel ill.

You must leave the bakery without buying anything else. Pay the baker his two copper coins for the buns and turn to **5**.

135

You approach the creature, asking him his business in helping you. He does not reply, but merely points skyward. You follow his gaze to the towering building from which you escaped. Clutches of crows sit huddled on the ivy-choked window ledges. One of them calls ominously. These are not ordinary birds; they are guardians of the tower. The black shapes suddenly take flight, heading straight towards the van in a dive-bombing formation that does not look friendly!

Without further questions, you grab hold of the grilles and hoist yourself into the back of the van. It takes off suddenly, reversing out of the alley and toppling the flower buckets. Water and flowers spray through the air as the van swerves into the street. You throw yourself upon the floor of the van.

Turn to **169**.

136

You realise there is nothing you can do for him. With a parting promise that you will not forget his help, you grab your satchel and take your leave.

Turn to **233**.

137

You explain hastily that you haven't enough money. The barmaid glares at you, then picks up the drink and tosses it into your face. You gasp in surprise, as nearby faeries turn to look at you and laugh.

'Can nun hold his spirut!' cries one.

You glance around for support, but there is none. It seems to be time to take your leave.

Turn to **186**.

138

The courtyard is fast becoming thick with smoke and flames. Choking from the foul air and hot wind, you dash towards the alleyway.

Turn to **11**.

139

You leave the herbalist's, feeling nervous. Your sense tells you it is best to be inside.

You may visit either the medicinary (turn to **85**) or the bakery (turn to **43**).

140

He introduces himself as Laer-Cyleric, a former teacher of Elder Magic. He explains that he was expelled from the Ordughadh – the Elder Fey order – for his unorthodox teaching methods. Nonetheless, he can still tell an Elder from a common fey, no matter what they might be wearing. He looks pointedly at your attire. He then reaches for an empty glass and begins to spin it idly on the table. His fingers dance across the rim, nimbly, almost invisibly. He breathes a word upon the glass and lets go. As it comes to a rest, upright, you see to your astonishment that it is now filled with a clear and golden liquid.

You stare at Cyleric in admiration. He shrugs.

'It maye be drinken,' he says, 'but it be nun the true drink. It be an illusion, a trick o' the eyes. It be the work of my pracktise o'er years, though I be nun talented. I be lepch-fey, half Elder Fey, half leprechaun, and leprechauns have nun the subtletie required for this magic.' Cyleric laughs to himself. 'Praye tell me, young feyling, what blood have ye? Elvin, perchance? Lutin? Or is it Mortal?'

You stare at Cyleric, unable to hide your unease. He laughs at you.

'Ye can nun work your magick, that be my guessen. Ye be owed teaching, for no matter what blood ye be, ye can nun cast spells until ye have passed the First Trial. In this, I can help ye, for I be a Laer – a teacher,' he says, reclining in his seat.

By the oily green light of the tavern lamps, you catch a glimpse of a knife blade, flashing beneath his cloak. You ask him what he wants in return. Although his face is dark, you can sense his smile.

'A drinkun,' he says.

Will you accept Cyleric's help (turn to **117**) or thank him and take your leave (turn to **210**)?

141

You enter the tunnel and begin to fumble your way forward in the dark. Your progress is slow, as you feel blindly for a path between the brambles. Your cloak protects you from the thorns, but there is nothing to protect your hands. They are soon scratched and pricked. You grimace against the pain and soldier on.

The pathway soon begins to slope upwards, and you can make out a sliver of light that marks the exit. You hurry on as fast as you can, keen to be free of the tunnel.

Make a note that you have been injured by the brambles, and turn to **165**.

142

You mutter the spell. The dwarf blinks heavily. His breathing deepens and you feel his grip loosen on your wrist. Though he has not quite fallen asleep, you are able to at least free yourself. Onlookers laugh and whistle.

'Next time ye will mind yer plæce, feyling,' says the dwarf, his words slurring.

You push your chair back and slip into the crowd, ignoring the jeers behind you.

Turn to **186**.

143

The figure shuffles inside the shop, bringing with it a wretched odour. You sidestep the creature, not wishing to look too closely at the rags, and quickly leave.

You hurry up the street, past the cluster of sleepy shops.

Will you seek refuge at the herbalist's shop (turn to 21) or hurry on to the bakery (turn to 43)?

144

You carve your triangle. Effie expels a breathy grunt as she examines your move. She carves her next cross. You see immediately that she has made a big mistake. There is only one move you need to make to win three triangles in a row.

Turn to 75.

145

These biscuits are highly nutritious. They are light enough to carry, and may be useful should you need a boost of energy.

The bannochs cost 1 copper each. If you would like to buy one, pay the baker now and return to **43**. If you have finished making your purchases, turn to **5**.

146

You run across the courtyard, following the statue-lined pathway. As you reach the tunnel, you hear the Air Elemental shrieking and the entrance door banging in the wind. Glancing back, you see the shape of spreading wings as the Elemental flies across the courtyard towards you!

Are you carrying a shamrock of any description? If you are, turn to **359**. If not, turn to **218**.

147

Looking wildly around, you see a nearby alleyway which may offer an escape. Alternatively, you could head back into the tunnel.

Will you choose the alleyway (turn to **138**) or the tunnel (turn to **158**)?

148

You try to shake free of Pearlie's grip, but she holds you tight.

'Young feyling!' she whispers, 'Ye think ye will nun be found soon enough, in suchlike garb?' She casts her eye over your clothes. 'These streets be the lair of Olcrada! If ye want to live the daye, comme with Pearlie. I give ye garb, show ye whot to do, little halven-fey.'

Her breath escapes her peeling lips, foul and stale. Her bloodshot eye peers around the edge of her cowl, surveying the street.

'Oobanata!' she cries suddenly. 'Vapour of the witch's brew! Comme with Pearlie! Comme now!'

Will you break free of Pearlie (turn to **128**) or follow her (turn to **252**)?

149

You ask the doctor if he knows where to find the Arch Warlock, telling him about the book that you need to deliver. The doctor regards you carefully.

'The Arch Warlock be the mæst powerful witch in Suidemor. His home be surrounded by cunnings and tricks, and he be ṇun easy to visit. I can tell ye this much: do nun climb the stone walls. I have treated many a broken bone for trying.'

Make a note of the doctor's advice. Would you like to buy something now (turn to **58**), or take your leave (turn to **226**)?

150

You follow the goblins into the lanes, your boots splashing in puddles of melted snow. You soon lose sight of them, though the sound of their laughter and footfalls leads you deep into a labyrinth of locked doors and barred windows. Towering buildings block the light, keeping the air cold and damp. At last you arrive in a dingy lane crowded with shops and traders. Twisted trees grow between the buildings, their branches bearing shop signs hung from chains or nails. You see the goblins disappear through the door of a grime-windowed tavern across the road.

You approach the tavern. A wooden sign above the door proclaims you to be at:

THE BRACKENROSE ARMS

You gaze at the sign in excitement. Pearlie had said the Blackrose Arms, you are sure, but the pigeon has led you here. It could hardly be a coincidence. Your thoughts are suddenly interrupted by the sound of soft cooing. You look down to see the pigeon, trembling in the gutter.

Do you have a bannoch biscuit (turn to **17**) or salve-all cream (turn to **2**)? If you have neither of these items, then there is nothing you can do for the pigeon and you must enter the tavern instead. Turn to **168**.

151

You hastily pull the bell. Tram gears grind underfoot as the tram slows. You pull the door open and jump to the cobblestone pavement below.

Turn to **222**.

152

'Nunn to fear, my dear!' she says.

Your sense tells you otherwise. You break free of her grip and dash into the street. Glancing about, you see that other shops are now open for business.

You may seek refuge at the herbalist's shop (turn to **21**), or the medicinary (turn to **85**).

153

You check your bag of geld.

If you need more geld and you would like to try Cyleric's spell again, you will need something to transform into coins. The following items may be transformed:

Toffee apples = 6 coppers
Geldwort seeds = 11 coppers

Cast the spell now if you have either of these items. You may create as many coins as you are able. If you have neither of these items, you will have to make do with any coins you still have.

Turn to **258**.

154

You stare at the letter in disbelief. Your father is alive, and he is the King of Suidemor! How can it be that for all these years your mother never told you? She claimed your father had died. If she sought to protect you, then what good has it done? For you are now in great danger, armed only with a single spell. You do not even have your spellbook any more, after your battle with the Elemental.

As if in reply to your thoughts, the door behind you is battered with sudden ferocity. The hinges shake, the wood splits and splinters. The talons of the Air

Elemental tear and scrape, and a draught of chilling air seeps through the fractures.

Quick! You must bind the parchment with the Ironring spell.

155

You follow the lane to the right, moving quickly in the darkness. Your cloak and boots are soon soaked through with rain. Behind you, the howling wind wreaks a path of destruction, snapping branches and tearing brambles from their roots. You know if you meet the Air Elemental again you will almost certainly die. Your heart floods with relief as you come upon the laneway by which you first entered, and at its end, the faithful church door.

Turn to 172.

156

You scramble backwards, tripping over an upturned chair and sprawling on the floor. Effie stands over you, a mountain of sagging flesh and foul odour. You brace yourself for her blow. Instead she lets out an enormous bellow of laughter, her broken teeth visible between mottled lips. She puckers and spits at you. The crowd cheer. Effie dismisses you with a wave of her fat hand and lumbers over to the bar. A few other patrons spit at you for good measure as you struggle to your feet, relieved at least to be alive.

Turn to **186**.

157

The door swings shut. You pull the bolt across and lean against the wood, shuddering with relief. You are not standing in the lane. Instead, you are in a small stone room. There are no windows, but a circle of light is cast from a single candle burning in a holder on the wall opposite. You wonder if this chamber will be your tomb. Yet, true to the Warlock's word, you see a simple wooden box resting on a shelf.

How many times will you open the box? Once (turn to **309**), twice (turn to **271**) or three times (turn to **351**)?

158

The courtyard is fast becoming thick with smoke and flames. Choking from the foul air and hot wind, you dash into the tunnel. Immediately you see that you have made a mistake, for waiting in the darkness is a strange and luminous vapour that appears to be floating towards

you. This is surely the 'oobanata' which so terrified the greeper, and you have run headlong into it! Though you try to run, your legs seem to have turn to lead. You watch helplessly as the vapour glides across the cobblestones towards you. Your knees buckle and you sink to the ground. The vapour touches your skin and coils around your limbs, and you feel your breath being sucked from you. You collapse into blackness...

Turn to **368**.

159

You utter the spell as the animal strikes. You are knocked to the ground and crushed by the great weight and heat of the beast which has fallen on you, apparently asleep! You shift yourself out from underneath and stagger to your feet. Pain flares in your shoulder. You glance down to see the torn fabric of your cloak and blood running down your arm. Nursing the wound, you hobble down the lane to safety.

Make a note that you have been injured by the dog, and turn to 230.

160

You approach the dwarf at his table. He glances up at you indifferently and continues eating. You take a seat at the other end of the table, feeling conspicuous without food or drink. On the dwarf's plate are the remains of a cooked bird sitting in a pool of grease. The dwarf sucks the meat off the last of the bones and mops up the fat with a chunk of bread.

Do you want to ask the dwarf if he knows anything about the Forgotten Spell (turn to 247), or make light conversation (turn to **110**)?

161

Though you would like to rest, there is precious little time. When the banshee's screams are sufficiently distant, you gather your reserves of courage and begin following the lane once more. It is all you can do to find the Warlock at this late hour.

You proceed slowly. The pathway begins to slope downwards, eventually coming to a set of stairs that leads into a tunnel, grown over and choked with dead brambles.

Navigating the tunnel in the dark will be dangerous. Do you have a candle? If you do, turn to 292. If not, turn to 141.

162

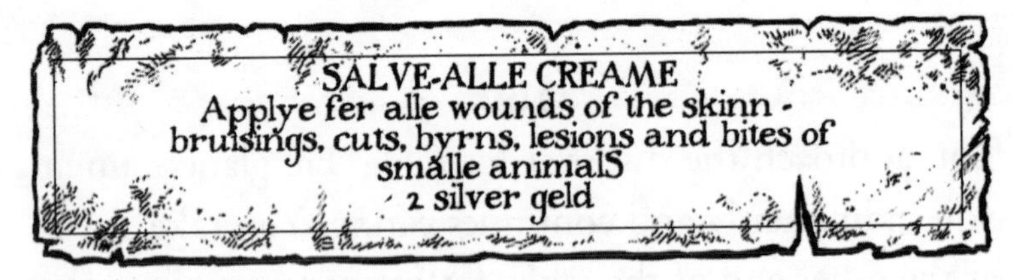

163

You run in Pearlie's direction, following her into the shadows of a lane. You catch sight of her slipping through a small door. As you duck under the frame, her crone's hand catches your shirt and pulls you into the darkness.

Turn to 201.

164

You glance across the road to the cluster of sleepy shops. Many of them are boarded up and dark within, though the glow from a few of the windows indicates they may be open for business.

Have you been stung by the poison nettles? If so, turn to **122**. If not, you may visit the bakery (turn to **43**), the herbalist (turn to **21**) or the medicinary (turn to **85**).

165

You step out from the tunnel. You are standing in a spacious garden surrounded by bramble-covered walls. A wide and weedy path lies before you, flanked by a row of life-sized statues, their bases buried in the overgrown lawn. The path leads to a courtyard on the far side of the garden, beyond which stands a many-storeyed building, its turrets choked by ivy. Surely this must be the Arch Warlock's home!

Were you injured in the lanes? If so, turn to the following numbers to find out the consequences for each injury you carry:

Bramble scratches – **240**
Dog maul – **188**
Magpie bite – **346**
Banshee curse – **364**
Frapella vine – **256**
If you were not injured, turn to **281**.

166

Ghoul's thistle is the only thing that will save you from the Unseelies. Though the plant seems odorless to you, it is quite pungent to the senses of these spirit creatures. Indeed, the apparitions gawp at you, then one by one they pull away. Heart pounding, you step back into the doorway. With a quick glance to the ground rushing by below, you jump. You land on the cobblestones, grazing your hands. At least you are alive, you acknowledge grimly, as you pick yourself up and hobble to the pavement.

Following the tramline, you continue along the pavement of cobblestones, hoping to blend in with the pedestrians. You walk under the faded awnings, passing shop windows displaying strange wares. Vendors vie for your custom but you keep your business to yourself and your eyes averted from their shrewd stares.

Gradually the shops diminish and are replaced with boarded-up doorways and broken windows. You pass few faeries; they keep their heads down, hurrying to their unimaginable destinations as the city darkens under a gauze of grey cloud.

Under the shelter of an eave, you pause to tighten your cloak about your shoulders. You are about to continue on your way when you hear a moaning coming from the doorway. You glance down to see a pale, groping hand emerging from what appears to be a bundle of rags on the ground. The hand, you notice, is missing three fingers. "Charitie!" breathes a miserable voice from beneath the rags.

Will you offer the creature something (turn to **78**), or quickly be on your way (turn to **219**)?

167

The tram rumbles past. Pieces of rotten fruit and other scraps are thrown at you from the windows. You run down the street as fast as you can, dodging pedestrians and ducking into a narrow lane.

Smack! Something hits you in the back of the head as you round the corner. Outraged, you turn to see a little black creature spinning through the air like a corkscrew and plummeting to a crash on the cobblestones. It lands on its backside with a yelp. Clutched in its claw-like hands is the goblin's purse! Little emerald eyes flash at you.

'I shares wyth ye half if ye open the clasp!' it squeaks, holding out the purse. You gape at the creature, amazed at its gall!

Will you help the imp (turn to **211**) or refuse him (turn to **192**)?

168

You push open the heavy, creaking door. The smell of cooked food and smoke greets your nostrils. It is lunch-time, and the tables of the Brackenrose Arms are filled with grisly-looking patrons. A crowd is gathered around the bar, watching a lively performance of a musician and a clown. The musician plays a fiddle while the clown juggles eggs in the air, smashing as many as he catches. The crowd boo and jeer at the performers, their glasses full and their faces drunken. Looking about the tables you see none that is empty. Of the lone patrons, there is a dwarf eating a meal, a drunken faery with his head on the table, and a large troll-like creature who is watching the show.

Examine the picture opposite. Would you like to approach the bar (turn to **41**), or sit at one of the tables? You may sit next to the dwarf (turn to **160**), the drunk (turn to **208**) or the troll (turn to **343**).

169

The van hurtles through a labyrinth of laneways. You hear the crows calling and swooping as you hug the floor and pray for your life. Tyres screech as the van sets a dare-devil pace around the corners. You are soon soaked and covered with petals and ripped leaves. The ride becomes extremely bumpy, the wheels flying over cobblestones. Then, just as suddenly, all is dark. The cries of the crows become distant and the van slows at last, and you realise that you are in some sort of tunnel.

Turn to **66**.

170

You consider how you are going to find the Blackrose Arms. With a heavy heart, you decide to brave the streets. You wrap your cloak close around you and are about to leave the lane when you hear the footfalls of running feet and shouting. You quickly press yourself into the shadows of the lane.

Turn to 200.

171

You follow the lane. It takes a sharp turn to the left, then right. Ahead you see a dead end, in the middle of which stands a rather gnarled, old tree. You notice that there are things dangling from the branches – necklaces and chains and pieces of colourful ribbon. At the base of the tree, shiny objects are strewn about – buttons, jewellery and even coins.

Would you like to help yourself to some coins (turn to 25), or go back to the junction (turn to 323).

172

You check the church door, but it is shut fast with an iron lock. You fumble for the keys given to you by the Warlock. In the faint light, you can see that each key has a rose engraved upon it. You stare numbly at the church door; in the wooden panel is also carved a rose.

You have but moments to spare. Only one of the keys will work. Choose the key that exactly matches the rose on the door and turn to that paragraph number to try it:

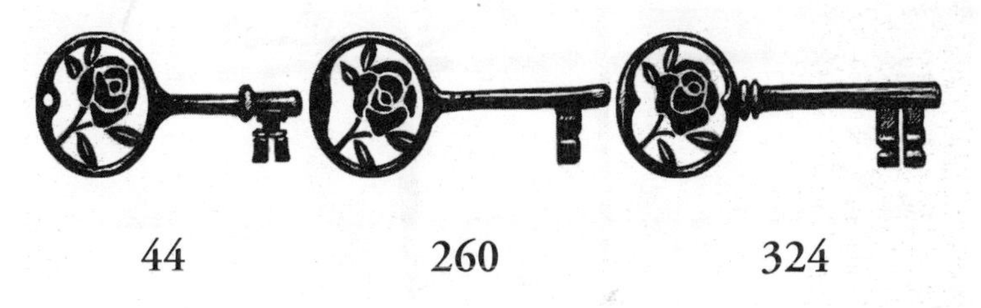

173

The imp clutches its spoils with clawed feet and takes off down the lane, somersaulting as it flies. You pack away your new possessions and head back to the street.

Turn to 222.

174

You carve your triangle roughly in the wood. Effie examines your move and carves a cross in reply. There is only one move you can make to stop her from getting three crosses in a row

Turn to 357.

175

You thank Garda for her help as she leads you through the shop to the door. She mumbles some magic at the lock and turns the handle, then pauses suddenly.

'Wait, halven! Ye can run me an errand in servyce fer these words.'

Garda shuffles over to a cluttered shelf and searches through the books. Dust falls from the shelves as she extracts book after book and discards them on the floor.

Coughing and muttering, she at last finds a small, thick volume bound in shiny red leather. She presses it into your hand.

'Deliver this booke to the Arch Warlock,' she says. 'He be waiting upon it, and though he be a witch, he be laerned of all thinges Elder.'

You read the title:

ŒЯЇГЇЮŞ ŒФ ЂЭ
ЂЇЯΨЫ ŒЮ LЭΨΨЭЯŞ
ŒФ ЂЭ ŞþŒЖЭЮ ШЫЯÐ

Garda unlocks the door.

'Ye came by the back entrance, though ye best take the front entrance to leave.' She mutters some magic and turns the latch. 'Go,' she says.

There is a number in the title of the book. You can use the faery alphabet in your spellbook to help you decipher it. Make a note of this number if you can find it, and turn to **100**.

176

The milk cart trundles down the street toward you, belching smoke into the morning air. Little faeries dash from the cart, shouldering bottles of milk, while in the driver's seat sits a figure hunched under a grey blanket, puffing on a pipe. You wave at him. He slows the cart and pokes out his features from the folds of the blanket.

'Best be inside, feyling. Oobanata, they be coming,' he calls out cryptically, pushing a lever into gear.

The faeries burst into a chorus of giggles as a smoky fart is discharged into the air. The cart trundles away.

Would you like to take the milkman's advice and seek refuge in the shops (turn to **164**), or would you like to try your luck in the alleyway (turn to **73**)?

177

You hold the items in your hand discreetly and utter the spell. You feel the coins materialising in your clenched fist. Sure enough, you have created authentic-looking coppers!

Turn to **258** to investigate the wares.

178

You catch the handrail and step onto the tram. Passengers fill the seats and aisles surrounded by luggage: rolls of material, battered boxes, pots of sickly plants, and infants tied in swathes of cloth. The tram appears to be a kind of travelling flea market. Chatter rises and falls amongst the sounds of clinking coins and distressed animals. A nearby goblin cradles a cage of finches, while chickens roam about freely, clucking and pecking at the dirty floor.

If you would like to buy something, turn to **153**. Otherwise, you can sit down next to the goblin (turn to **243**), or find a discreet place to stand (turn to **330**).

179

You wend your way through the crowd, looking for somewhere to sit.

Will you sit next to the dwarf (turn to **160**), the drunk (turn to **208**) or the troll (turn to **343**)?

180

You try to prise the tin from the imp's fiendish grip.

'Mine! Mine!' screams the imp, flinging himself at you and sinking his teeth into your ankle.

Crying out in pain, you shake him off, sending him cart-wheeling across the cobblestones. With a few strides you are upon him. You bring your boot down on the tin purse angrily. This time it is the imp who cries out in pain. He releases the tin and scrambles free, loping away on injured limbs. You watch him go, your ankle aching.

Do you have any salve-all cream? If you do, you may salve the wound now without repercussion. Otherwise, you may find at some stage that your magical powers are impaired by the poison of this creature's bite. Make a note that you have been bitten by an imp, and turn to 207.

181

You return from the bar carrying the drinks. As you approach the table, you are alarmed to see Cyleric leafing through your spellbook! You should not have left your satchel unattended! Cyleric sees your expression and grins.

'It be merely a booke of elementary spells,' he sneers. 'Of nun use to me. However-it-be, I do find some measure of interest in *this* …'

He holds up the piece of parchment sent to you by the Elder Oeda, revealing the writing in the lamplight.

'The Forgotten Spell … It be nun the magick of the Elder Fey, nor of the Witches, for it be the magick of *both*, and mæst evil and potent besides. It be lost now, knowen to nun save one fey… the Arch Warlock of Suidemor.'

Your heart leaps at Cyleric's news.

'I must find him!' you say, your anger forgotten.

Cyleric, it seems though, does not share your excitement. He shrugs.

'The Arch Warlock's home be at the Blackrose Coven,' he tells you. 'It be at the end of the tramline – just simpelie follow the tracks.'

He drops the parchment in a puddle of spilt liquor. You snatch it up. Pearlie was right about Blackrose after all! Cyleric takes up his glass and drinks from it in one swill. His eyes, you fancy, are glazed as he leans towards you.

'I be a vagrant now, a thiefing drunk wunce a teacher. But let me tell ye this: there be naught ye can do fer the King, fer even if ye find the spell, what wyll ye do with it? Your quest, halven-fey, will fail. Suidemor will protect ye in the daye, but nun of nyght, when alles be dark and the devyces of magick strongest. Ye ought flee the city by nightfalle or be found dead ere the morne.'

His words press heavily on your heart. He slumps suddenly in his seat, affected by the liquor, you guess. It seems you have gleaned all you can from him. He sits with his shoulders hunched over the table, his wings again pallid, cloaking his thin shoulders.

Will you offer him something from your satchel as a parting gift (turn to 27) or leave him be (turn to 136)?

182

You close the door and head back down the lane in the opposite direction.

Turn to 195.

183

The quill feather comes from the blue-winged owl, a very rare and beautiful bird, according to the vendor. The nib is set in gold and looks to be of some craftsmanship.

Return to 258.

184

You carve your triangle. Effie expels a breathy grunt as she examines your move. She carves her next cross. You see immediately that she has made a big mistake. There is only one move you need to make to win three triangles in a row.

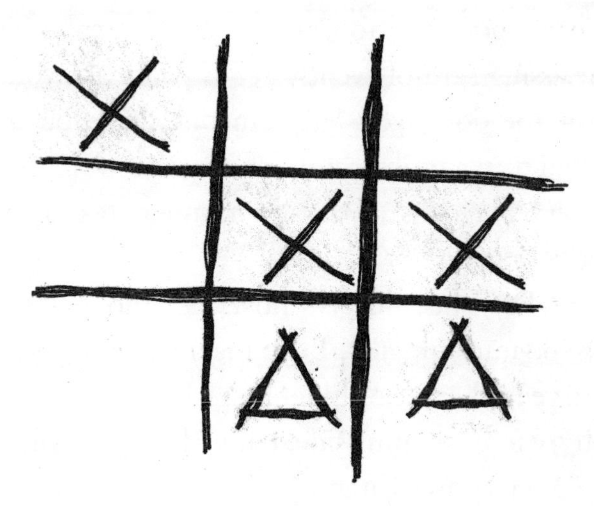

Turn to 75.

185

The Elemental spreads its wings as it approaches, snorting at the rain and blowing out steamy breath. Up close you can smell its sweating body and matted fur, intermingled with the smell of your own fear. With the creature towering over you, you sink to the ground and slide underneath its belly. The Elemental lashes out in confusion. You feel a deadly talon slice across the flesh of your back and a searing pain, before you slither free and break into a terrified run back down the lane.

Make a note that you have been struck by an Air Elemental and turn to **51**.

186

You have no wish to stay in the tavern after the embarrassing turn of events. Yet as you make your way towards the door, you feel someone grab you on the arm. You turn angrily, coming face to face with a bleary-eyed faery. He looks at you for a moment, taking in your garb and presence.

'Elder Fey,' he whispers hoarsely, 'though to mine eyes ye be nun initiated. Buye me a drinkun and I will initiate ye in the arte of Elder magick.'

You try to push him aside, telling him you don't have any geld. His grip tightens.

'Elder Fey, be ye not? Have ye trouble with magick? Inabilitie to casten spells? Whenne we be finished,' he promises drunkenly, 'ye will nun need geld.'

Will you accept the drunk's offer (turn to **237**) or would you prefer to be rid of him (turn to **10**)?

187

You turn and sprint across the chamber, running blindly into the hallway. Near the door, you trip over an obstacle. Panic fills your mind as you realise that you have tripped over the dead priest. You scramble to your feet and reach for the door…

A terrifying screech fills the air. You turn to see the silhouette of the Air Elemental launching itself down the hallway. It is upon you within seconds. Deadly talons rip into your flesh. You slump to the ground, the smell of your own blood and death rising about you.

Turn to 332.

188

Your shoulder is throbbing painfully and you can no longer ignore it.

If you have any feverfew flowers or salve-all cream, you may use them now to treat your injuries and suffer no consequences. Otherwise, you must keep an eye out for a cure. Until you find a cure, you will be unable to cast any spells. If you have any other injuries to attend to, return to 165. Otherwise, turn to 281.

189

You cross the road, heading towards the shop.

Were you stung by the nettles in the prison? If you were, turn to 77. If not, turn to 43.

190

You carve your triangle. Effie's beady eyes flash excitedly. She carves a cross in the centre of the squares, then leans back with folded fleshy arms to watch. You see immediately that you have made a big mistake.

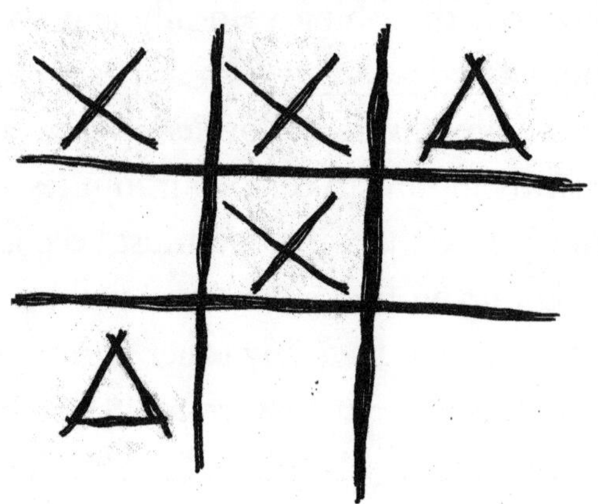

Turn to 26.

191

With your added strength, you run through the whipping wind. Glancing back, you see the waterhag rising from the water, her bloated skin dripping weeds and slime. You do not wait to see any more.

Turn to 314.

192

You turn your back on the imp. He flings himself after you, sinking his claws into your ankle. Crying out in pain, you shake him off, sending him cart-wheeling across the cobblestones. With a few strides you are upon him. You bring your boot down on the purse angrily. This time it is the imp who cries out in pain. He releases the purse and scrambles free, loping away on injured limbs. You watch him go, your ankle aching.

Do you have any salve-all cream? If you do, you may salve the wound now without repercussion. Otherwise, you may find that your magical powers are impaired by the poison of this creature's bite. Make a note that you have been bitten by an imp, and turn to **326**.

193

This lane is wide and relatively free of brambles, so you walk for some distance unhindered. After a while you hear the sound of running water, and you soon come upon a grotto, built into the dead end of a stone wall. Water falls over the lip of a birdbath into a pool at the base. Ferns and mosses spill over the rocks. It is a very peaceful place. Indeed, a stone seat has been built next to the pond for travellers to rest.

Would you like to rest for a moment (turn to **232**) or return to the junction (turn to **314**)?

194

The doctor swabs your wounds with a pungent oil, muttering a string of strange words as he works. You grit your teeth against the pain as he binds your wounds in a bandage. At last it seems your treatment is over. The doctor shuffles to the shelves at the back of the shop. Dust stirs as his cloak trails on the floor. He returns with three little jars held in his thin, cupped hands.

'Yer wounds tell of danger,' he says gravely. 'Ye maye be wyse to buy some aids for yer journey.'

Make a note of this paragraph number, then turn to the numbers on the jars to read the labels. The cream and elixir each cost two silver coins. The eye ointment costs one gold coin. Buy as many as you like (or none at all), and then turn to 226.

195

You walk some distance, your footsteps crunching on dead leaves and fallen twigs. The air is still, this lane as deserted as the last. You quicken your pace, following the lane as it twists and turns.

Up ahead, there is a tree growing in the middle of the lane. It is a peculiar sight, for though it is winter, this tree is covered in greenery and heavy with fruit. The smell of citrus fills the air. The tree is enclosed by a white picket fence, and standing under it is a young girl of about your age, wearing a tattered-looking dress. She is picking oranges and putting them in a basket which she holds on her hip. Under the tree grows fresh green grass, and on a nearby branch, a bird hops about, singing prettily.

You draw close, and the girl turns to stare at you. She smiles, wiping her brow with her arm and glancing up at the sky.

'Looks likely to be rain,' she says. 'I had best be inside or the Warlock will be angry.'

She steps towards you, bare feet on the grass, carrying the heavy basket in both hands.

'Will ye open the gate for me?' she asks, indicating a small gate in the picket fence.

Will you open the gate for the girl (turn to **215**) or ignore her request and be on your way (turn to **310**)?

196

Leaving the merchants to their wares, you move through the crowded tram.

Did you buy an owl-feather quill? If you did, turn now to 54. If not, turn to 299.

197

You decline the drink, offering it instead to the dwarf. He shrugs and finishes off the second glass. His cheeks are glowing red and he appears quite drunk. He resumes his meal with hearty relish.

Now would be a good time to ask him about the Forgotten Spell – turn to 282.

198

You find Garda standing at the stove, stirring gruel in a saucepan and attending to a kettle of boiling water. You set the books down, exhausted. Morning light fights through the gaps in the window drapes, tinged, you fancy, with sunshine. Your spirits raise a little, as Garda brings you a steaming bowl of some thick and lumpy substance and a cup of strong-smelling tea. You sink into an armchair and accept the food gratefully.

'It be foul-tasting fodder but goodlie enough,' she says.

Garda reaches down for the pile of books, then pauses, staring at them in utter amazement.

'Ye did finden it,' she whispers, picking up the third and smallest book – a thin volume bound in frayed blue cloth. 'This booke be blank ... the writings be nun read by common fey, nun the insides nore the outsides. If ye did finden it, then there be but one answer to the riddle: ye have the Elder Fey sight – indeed, ye be Elder Fey.'

Garda stares at you, somewhat in awe. You remember the strange blank book in your satchel, and the message on the parchment that was blown from your hands.

Will you show Garda the book (turn to **99**) or hide your knowledge (turn to **88**)?

199

The Darkward spell was your last defence. A triumphant shriek fills the air as deadly talons tear through your flesh. You slump to the ground, the smell of your own blood and death rising about you.

Turn to 332.

200

From your hiding place, you see a flock of pigeons fly into the lane, followed by a pair of goblins chasing them. The birds take flight to the safety of the window ledges and balustrades above, leaving the goblins to curse and snatch at the air. On the ground, a solitary pigeon lopes along the cobblestones, unable to fly. One of the goblins shrieks and lunges at the bird, catching the creature in his outstretched hands. Your heart leaps as you think of Pearlie's words:

'Make one allowance to follow a pigeon with a broken wing …'

Will you confront the goblins (turn to **89**) or secretly cast a spell?

201

You are led through a dank corridor and down a staircase, enveloped at last by a black, airless space. A door shuts. Pearlie begins to incant, 'fiere aire weter earden norde este suide weden …'

The minutes pass. At long last, Pearlie stops. You hear her breathing as she moves about. A lantern is lit and light suddenly spreads into the room like melted butter, revealing a tiny room of cluttered furniture. It seems that everything Pearlie owns is stuffed into it: broken chairs, odd cups and saucers, bundles of rags and a stained mattress for a bed. The back wall of the room is partitioned by a brocaded curtain, once fine but now moth-eaten. Pearlie disappears behind the curtain and returns bearing a bundle of clothes.

'Ye be from the Mortal wyrld, I ken. I been there, I seen Mortals dressed as ye be. This – to chænge yer garb,' she says, holding the bundle out to you.

You follow her instructions wordlessly, pulling on a pair of battered boots and a cloak of wispy, grey fibre. Pearlie is pleased.

'Coal fibres,' she explains, touching the cloak. 'Whot the factorie feylings wear, after they have their wings cut off...'

She grins, revealing the sheen of her fleshy lips. Her gaze falls to your leather satchel. Before you can protest, she snatches the satchel and spreads your belongings all over the table. Your heart sinks as she picks up the spellbook and flicks through the pages.

'Invisiblie words ...' she mutters.

She tosses the book aside and extracts from the folds of her rags a crumpled bit of parchment. She shoves it at you. You are startled to see it is the note given to you by the greeper, on behalf of the Elder Oeda.

'I did finden this scrap o' paper,' she says. 'It be washed up in a gutter hereabouts, nothing more than scrap to some, but Pearlie ken it be invisiblie. Readen it to Pearlie,' she impresses, her eye turned on you, gleaming excitedly.

Will you read the message (turn to 236), or hide its meaning (turn to 278)?

202

A favourite of many creatures, these potent sweets are far from nutritious, but their sugar content alone may be of some benefit should you find yourself hungry.

You may buy a bag of toffee apples if you have two copper coins. Pay the baker and return to 43. If you have finished making your purchases, turn to 5.

203

There are eight teeth in the bag.

You may turn the teeth into coppers (cast the geld spell now) or keep them as they are for later use (return to 258).

204

You walk under the arbour, following the path as it curves around. It is strangely pleasant, with the ground spongy underfoot and the perfume of flowers wafting in the air. You have not gone far when you find yourself stopping to admire the blooms. Their scent is delicious. You breathe in deeply, feeling warm and happy. Perhaps you could just lie down for while, as a rest would surely do you good …

You are falling asleep! Do you have any vivifying elixir (turn to 241)? If not, turn to 14.

205

You carve your triangle. Effie expels a breathy grunt as she examines your move. She carves her next cross. You see immediately that she has made a big mistake. There is only one move you need to make to win three triangles in a row.

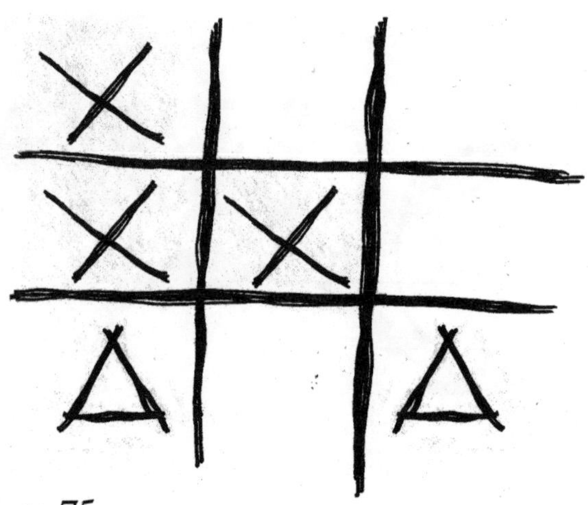

Turn to 75.

206

You find your coppers can buy a strong liquor for Cyleric and a milder tonic for yourself, with one coin left over as change.

Make a note of your change and turn to **181**.

207

With the imp gone, you inspect the tin. It is made of sturdy metal. Inside is a potent, ground tobacco of a deep yellow colour. You can see no immediate use for it, though it is light enough to carry should you want to keep it.

You may now search through the possessions abandoned by the imp. If there is anything you haven't investigated, do so now. Remember to keep a note of this paragraph number, so you can return after each investigation.

Silver coins (turn to **349**).

A box of matches (turn to **12**).

A pressed shamrock (turn to **307**).

When you have finished, turn to **268**.

208

You approach the table, set at the back of the tavern in the shadows where the light from the oil lamps does not reach. The drunk lies with his arms in a puddle of drink, his wings covering his shoulders like drapes of worn, silken material.

You ease yourself into a chair, trying not to wake him. He stirs and mutters in his sleep. His hand gropes on the table, his long, thin fingers finding an empty glass and knocking it to the floor. He snaps awake, his wings rippling to life, and looks at you with bleary eyes.

'Elder Fey,' he whispers hoarsely, taking in your garb and presence. 'Though to mine eyes ye be nun initiated … 'Tis strange and rare, though it be possible in these darkened dayes ... Have ye trouble with magick? Inabilitie to casten spells?'

He glances around secretively, then whispers, 'Buye me a drinkun and I will initiate ye in arte of Elder magick.'

You begin to tell him you don't have any geld, but he raises his finger to silence you.

'Whenne we be finished, ye will nun need geld,' he says with a wink.

Turn to **140**.

209

You quickly duck through the shop, murmuring your thanks to Hensoi as you pass and keeping your eyes averted. You sidestep the creature, not wishing to look too closely at the rags. A short but terrible laugh escapes her lips as you exit into the street.

Turn to **139**.

210

Pushing the glass away, you tell Cyleric that you have an important errand to run and you must be on your way. As you thank him for his time, he grabs you by the wrist.

'By no mistake,' he whispers, his breath sour with liquor, 'ye be in danger. Your guise does nun fool the trained eye, and there be many who wyll want to murder ye, if for naught than to laye their hands on your belongings which be likely worthe more than your life.'

Cyleric tightens his grip.

'Even a dullard could choke ye with bare hands. Ye be defenceless without magick.'

He releases his grip. Cyleric is right, you realise. You are lucky to be alive even now. You must accept his help or likely perish alone.

Turn to **117**.

211

You agree to help the imp, though you are wary of his sharp claws as he relinquishes his prize. He watches you, salivating and hopping about as you undo the buckle and distribute the contents on the ground.

You may share the contents with the imp. Keep a note of this paragraph number in order to return to it after investigating your chosen items. Choose two of the following:

Silver coins (turn to **349**).
A box of matches (turn to **12**).
A pressed shamrock (turn to **307**).
A tin of snuff (turn to **363**).

When you have chosen your items, turn to **173**.

212

You carve your triangle roughly in the wood. Effie examines your move and carves a cross in reply. There is only one move you can make to stop her from getting three crosses in a row.

Turn to 239.

213

Hoping you have the correct order for the bowls, you sup from the ones you need. The liquid is warm and nourishing. When you are finished, the Warlock nods sagely.

''Tis time then to tell ye of greater affairs, and to help ye with yer quest,' he says.

The broth has lifted all curses and healed all wounds, including a crow's peck. You may now cast your spells as required.

Turn to 250.

214

You push the door open and step through into another, slightly larger, lane. Looking left, then right, you find no signs to indicate which way to go.

If you have a compass, turn to 80. If you do not, you will have to rely on luck and intuition to navigate this maze. Would you like to go left (turn to 244), or right (turn to 65)?

215

You open the latch and the gate flies open. A shriek fills the air as the girl crosses the threshhold of the gate and transforms into the tallest woman you have ever seen, with hair like thick plaits of rope and a face as white as a corpse. The basket of oranges spills into the lane as she raises her hands and laughs into the wind, wild and terrifying.

This creature is a banshee. You will need added strength to escape it. If you have some falliard bread, you may eat it now and choose to either run (turn to 337) or cast a spell. If you do not have any falliard bread, you must face your foe with nothing but courage (turn to 353).

216

The ring is of simple craftsmanship, forged of a tarnished tin and bearing a small green-stone shamrock as a centrepiece. It is quite pretty, if not particularly valuable.

Make a note that you are carrying a shamrock, and return to 258.

217

The Elemental advances, snorting at the rain and blowing out steamy breath. It seems somewhat uncertain of your power, as you are still protected by the Darkward spell. You may, however, be too tired to cast any more magic.

If you have any falliard bread, you may eat some now and try to cast a spell. Otherwise, you may have to resort to physical combat. If you have a knife, turn to **130**. If not, you are defenceless and you must either try to dodge the Elemental (turn to **185**), or climb the wall (turn to **342**).

218

The creature is upon you within seconds. In your fear, the Darkward spell slips from your command. It is your last defence. Deadly talons tear through your flesh. A triumphant shriek fills the air, accompanied by your final valiant cry as you slump to the ground, the smell of your own blood and death rising about you.

Turn to **332**.

219

You close the spellbook, aware of Garda watching you.

'Dun trusten no fey in this city, halven,' she warns. 'It be ruled by the Elder Fey in name only, for the King Othirom has not been seen for many a year and the castle is locked to all. It be the King's brother, Olcrada, who rules in truth. He commands a magick far stronger than Elder magic alone, for he has learnt the secrets of Witcherie, the only magick to rival that of the Elder Fey. With the power of both, he surely plots to take the throne. Ai! 'Tis the petty squabble of brothers that brings the city to ruin!'

Garda huffs angrily as she gathers up the breakfast dishes, dumping them with a clatter into the sink. She then tosses a grubby leather pouch at you.

'That be payement for yer work,' she says.

You open the pouch to find twelve coins: seven copper, three silver and one gold.

'Where should I go?' you ask, feeling none too cheered.

Garda looks at you, her face hardening.

'Ye be escaping frum magickal forces, I ken, and alles I knoweth is the magickal forces will nun be finding ye here. Ye must leave now, before ye bring yer blackened fortune to my shoppe.'

She snuffs out the candle beside the armchair. The smell of acrid wax fills the air.

Make a note of the coins you have. Do you want to ask Garda if she knows of the Forgotten Spell (turn to **93**) or thank her and take your leave (turn to **175**)?

220

Leaving the orange tree behind, you proceed slowly, following the lane. The pathway begins to slope downwards, eventually coming to a set of stairs that leads into a tunnel, grown over and choked with dead brambles.

It is going to be dangerous navigating the tunnel in the dark. Do you have a candle? If you do, turn to 292. If not, turn to 141.

221

You ask the barmaid if she has heard of the Forgotten Spell. She blinks, poker-faced, then tells you sharply to move along if you have nothing to buy.

Do you want to buy a drink (turn to 62), or leave the bar and sit at one of the tables (turn to 179)?

222

You follow the street, keeping the tramline in sight. This part of the city is eerily deserted. High, stone walls line the pavements, strangled by weeds and winter-bare vines. Broken signs point to darkened lanes. A chill wind reminds you of the task ahead and your pace quickens.

At length you see the end of the tramline. Beyond lies a dead end: a ten-foot wall of stone. You approach the wall and examine it. There is no entrance to speak of, but there is an engraving on one of the stones, which reads:

Blackrose
The Coven of the
Arch Warlock of Suidemor

Welcome, friend

Do you want to try knocking (turn to **348**), try climbing the wall (turn to **301**) or try casting a spell?

223

You push your chair back, readying yourself to run. Effie stands up. Onlookers gape while the parrot squawks, 'Fight! Fight!' It is obvious you are going to be squashed by this troll unless you do something fast!

Do you want to run (turn to **156**) or cast a spell?

224

Trying your luck with one of these treats proves to be a bad idea, for no sooner have you bitten into the sugary coating than your mouth is filled with a bitter, gooey substance which makes you feel quite ill. The baker smiles faintly and perhaps with some satisfaction at the expression on your face as you try to swallow the horrible goo.

You cannot stomach the thought of trying something else. You must pay the baker one silver geld and turn to **5**.

225

You examine the arbour. The vines writhe under your hands as you try to part them, quickly enclosing any spaces you make. Glancing back at the door, you see the thick stems creeping over the wooden panelling, trapping you!

You will have to walk under the arbour (turn to **204**).

226

You utter your thanks to the doctor and turn to leave. The shop door swings open suddenly. A chill wind blows in as a bedraggled figure clothed in rags steps into the doorway. A plume of misted breath escapes the creature, dissipating in the warm shop. Your skin prickles in fear.

''Tis Pearlie, Doktor,' comes a rasping voice. 'After some medicinnes, as others be.'

Have you seen Pearlie in another shop? If so, turn to **242**. If not, turn to **143**.

227

You utter the spell. The teeth turn into eight shiny coppers.

If you would like to make more purchases, return to **258** and select from the items. If you would prefer to keep the money, turn to **196**.

228

You slip the keys into the pocket of your cloak, barely daring to breathe as you watch the handle turn and the door open. A thick, purple tendril oozes through the gap and feels its way across the carpet of moss. The Warlock bears his staff aloft and begins to chant in a terrifying voice. Under his command, the oobanata retreats to the doorway like a whimpering dog.

'Where lurks your master, Olcrada?' booms the Warlock, furious. 'Goe back to him and delyver this message:

that the Arch Warlock of Suidemor shall reap revenge for this invasion! GOE!'

At that moment, the sound of shattering glass fills the chamber. You tear your eyes from the door to see the windows breaking, one after the other. Fragments of glass are showered across the floor. Oobanata tendrils glide over the broken panes. Wind swirls around you and the lanterns are blown out, plunging you into darkness before the Warlock's staff flares, the end of it glowing with a great ball of light. He begins to incant, his voice thunderous and powerful, yet his eyes widen in horror as he sees the oobanata slithering at his feet. He stumbles backwards, clutching at his chest with one hand. The light sparks and flickers, glowing a hallowed green before fading like an ember, as the Warlock drops the staff and sinks to his knees.

Do you wish to cast a spell, or wait to see what happens (turn to 262)?

229

You insert the key. The tumblers click. You unlatch the door and pull it open upon a scene of horror. The Elemental crouches before you, haunches glistening with sweat. Before you have time to react, icy breath envelops you as the creature attacks. Talons tear into your flesh. A triumphant shriek fills the air, accompanied by your final valiant cry as you slump to the ground, the smell of your own blood and death rising about you, before a curtain of darkness is pulled over your eyes …

Turn to **332**.

230

You hurry on, glancing uneasily up at the forboding clouds, dreading both the encroaching night and the storm it will bring. You follow the lane as it slopes downwards into the mouth of a tunnel, overgrown with weeds and dead brambles.

Navigating the tunnel in the dark will be dangerous. Do you have a candle? If you do, turn to **292**. If not, turn to **141**.

231

Hoping you have the correct order for the bowls, you sup from the ones you think you need. The Warlock watches you grimly. Your attempt to guess was as brave as it was doomed. You feel a sudden stab of pain in your stomach. You cry out, doubling over on the mossy floor as the pain stabs again.

'Fool ye nun with the powers of Witcherie,' intones the Arch Warlock, 'fer death be the penance.'

Sure enough, as the pain wracks your body, your vision fails and you fall into darkness…

Turn to **368**.

232

You sit on the seat, relieved to be resting beside the soothing water. After a moment, however, you realise the water has stopped gurgling. An eerie silence settles over the grotto. A breeze stirs the little ferns. You take up your satchel uneasily, just as a gust of wind enters the grotto, bringing with it leaves and debris. You wrap your cloak tightly around you as the wind swirls, growing stronger and stronger. You try to press against the wind, but it pushes you back. You notice then that something is happening to the birdbath. The water is churning and you watch in horror as a revolting, fleshy hand emerges from the muck and grasps the lip of the bowl. The hand is bloated, twice the size of your own, and you do not want to find out who it belongs to!

If you want to run, you will need extra energy. If you have some falliard bread, you may eat it now and outrun the waterhag (turn to **191**). Otherwise, you must cast a spell now.

233

You step outside the tavern into the busy street. A wintry sun fights its way down through bare branches and sagging rooftops, warming your face. You wrap your cloak around you and hoist your satchel on your shoulder. As you do so, you notice how light it feels. A flutter of fear turns your stomach as you untie the leather straps. Sure enough, all your belongings are missing, save your spellbook.

Infuriated, you push your way back into the tavern. The table where you were sitting is vacant. Your heart sinks.

Were you carrying a book from Garda Grye for the Arch Warlock? If you were, add the number on the book to this paragraph number and turn to the result. If you don't have the book, turn to 277.

234

You give Effie the bag, embarrassed by the jeers and whistles of the onlookers. Effie spits at you as you take your leave, causing more laughter as you push your way through the crowd.

Turn to **186**.

235

A small, compact loaf of magical goodness. Just one slice will increase your stamina, strength and abilty to cast spells.

You may buy a slice of this bread if you have a gold coin. Make a note of this purchase and return to 43. If you have finished making your purchases, turn to 5.

236

You read the message aloud. Pearlie leans close.

'The Forgotten Spell ...' she breathes. 'It be the spell casted upon the King Othirom. Make him forgetten alles – even his great Mortal love, whom they sayeth did bear his only childe. But of this he remembers naught, and carries œnly a raven-black sadness in his heart. Soon he will die of this sadness ... is already dying, most surely.'

She prods you hard with a finger.

'The King's brother Olcrada keepeth watch over the city frum his tower. Ai! Ye wyll nun live in this city long enough to find ye bearings, let alone the spell! The oobanata – they come sometimes at daye, *always* at nyght. Those they kill be chænged to Air Elementals, creatures of wind and wile. Ye best leave the city ere nightfalle if ye dun want to meet one.'

Pearlie laughs, a horrible rasping sound. You begin to pick up your belongings nervously.

'Ah, halven,' she says, more softly, 'perhappen yer destinie will be blessed. Let Pearlie read yer fortune. That be whot Pearlie does.'

Pearlie's fortune-telling will usually cost one gold coin, but she will trade any token with you, be it coin, food, herb or medicine. If you would like to pay for Pearlie's services, turn to 257. If you don't want to pay Pearlie, turn to 47.

237

With reservations, you allow the faery to lead you away from the door towards a table at the back of the tavern where the light from the oil lamps does not reach. He offers you a chair at the table, cluttered by empty drinking glasses. You slide into the chair, clutching your satchel close.

Turn to **140**.

238

You utter the spell under your breath. Though you mean to instil fear in the goblins, instead the pigeon starts squawking, blind with panic. The goblins stare suspiciously at the bird. They cast their gaze about the shadowed lane. From their belts, they each remove a short-handled knife.

Will you make your presence known (turn to **48**), or stay hidden in the shadows (turn to **127**)?

239

You carve your triangle. Effie's beady eyes flash excitedly. She carves a cross in the centre of the squares, then leans back with folded, fleshy arms to watch. You see immediately that you have made a big mistake.

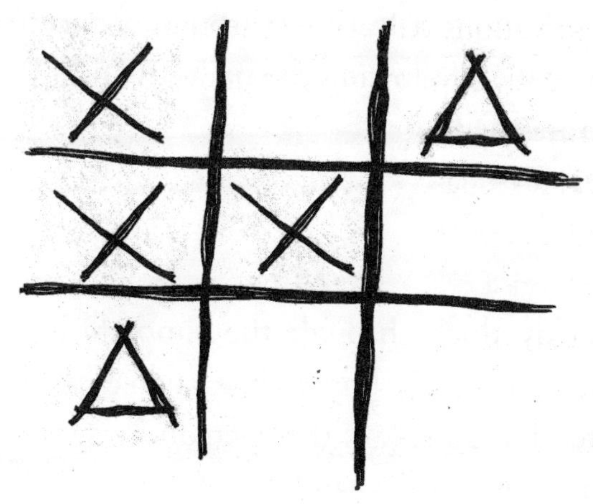

Turn to **26**.

240

Rose brambles are poisonous, and the longer you leave your wounds untreated, the sooner you will find yourself sick with fever.

If you have any feverfew flowers, you may use them now to treat your injuries and suffer no consequences. Otherwise, you must keep an eye out for a cure. Until you find a cure, you will be unable to cast any spells. If you have any other injuries to attend to, return to **165**. Otherwise, turn to **281**.

241

You open your satchel and find the vial. Though sleepiness is overcoming you, you manage to put the vial to your lips and drink. A bolt of coldness suddenly runs through your belly. You snap awake and scramble to your feet. You must leave the arbour at once! You run under the vines, following the pathway until you come at last to another door.

Turn to **214**.

242

You quickly duck through the shop, feeling Pearlie watching you. A short but terrible laugh escapes her lips. As you reach the safety of the open doorway, she catches your wrist with her icy hand.

''Tis only Pearlie!' she rasps at you.

Turn to **148**.

243

You take a seat beside the goblin, who flashes you an unfriendly look. The finches in the cage hop on overcrowded wooden perches.

'One gold geld apiece,' advises the goblin, the smell of his stale breath wafting through cracked lips. You quickly look away, ignoring him. The gears of the tram grind underfoot as it rumbles forward.

Through the grimy window you watch the lanes and

streets passing by. Gradually the shops diminish and are replaced with boarded-up doorways and broken windows. Faeries hurry to their unimaginable destinations as the city darkens under a gauze of grey cloud.

Suddenly, the goblin beside you lets out a holler. He dumps the cage of finches on the floor, springs to his feet and points at you.

'Thiefe!' he cries.

Passengers shift in their seats to look at you.

'Common feyling, stœle my purse! Arresten this fey!' cries the goblin.

You hear a cry of support from the onlookers, and a quick glance about the tram tells you there is no shortage of passengers willing to arrest you. You jump from your seat and make for the door. As you reach the railing you feel your legs suddenly freeze. The goblin is pointing a bony finger at you and muttering a string of words. To your alarm, you find you cannot move your legs at all!

You are going to have to do something fast. You have time enough to try one spell only. If your spell doesn't work, you must turn to **283**.

244

You continue on for a short distance, coming to another lane on your right.

Would you like to go right (turn to **193**), or continue on (turn to **269**)?

245

You utter the spell and the parchment transforms in your hand, the paper crackling and spitting as it reverts to common metal. You slip the ring quickly on your finger. Taking a deep breath, you face the door for the third time. Carved in the wood is a third rose, still intact, even as the wood bends and buckles from the blows of the Elemental. You pray the door will open to something other than your death.

Check the rose insignia for the last time and match it to a key.

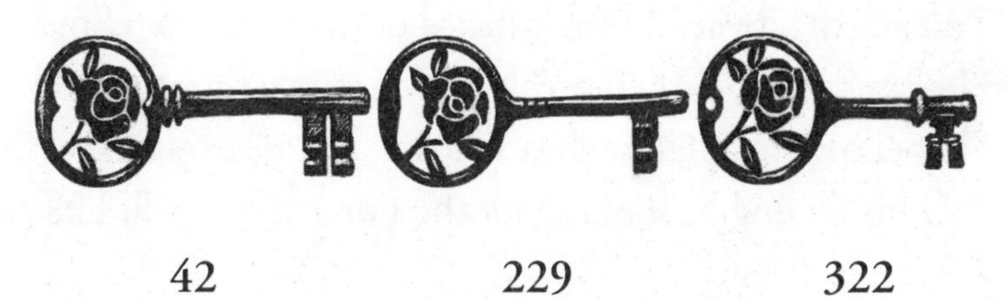

42 229 322

246

You utter the spell just as the banshee woman turns on you, her face glowing. She points her finger at you, then suddenly recoils. She screams again and floats off down the lane, arms flailing.

Relieved to be alive, you listen to her screams until they have faded. After a time you gather your reserves of courage and begin following the lane once more. Though you have escaped the banshee, you dread to think what other creatures may be waiting for you in the lanes of the Blackrose Coven.

Turn to 220.

247

You ask the dwarf if he has heard of the Forgotten Spell. He gawps at you, then breaks out in sputtering laughter. He bellows to a fellow dwarf sitting at a nearby table.

'This feyling be looking fer the Forgotten Spell. Have ye seen it, friend?'

More laughter breaks out around you.

You glance about, alarmed at the attention you are beginning to draw. The dwarf suddenly grabs your arm. His fingers dig painfully into your skin.

'If ye be searching fer spells,' he says, 'then yer guise conceales yer arte. Prove yer magickcræft.'

You may try to cast a spell for the dwarf, or wrest yourself free (turn to 38).

248

You sidestep the mess and continue along the lane.

Turn to 230.

249

You wait, your breath frosting in the cold morning air. At last the shadow of a figure appears behind the glass. A latch clicks and the door creaks open, revealing a cloaked faery with a willowy beard. He greets you with a phlegmy cough.

'Have ye an appointun?' he asks wheezily.

You shake your head and his gaze narrows.

'Comme,' he says, standing aside for you.

You step inside the shop. It is cool and dingy, and smells strongly of sulphur and other medicines. Acrid candles burn along the shelves beside glass jars and bottles of different coloured liquids. The doctor pulls the stub of a candle off the shelf and inspects your wounds by the light of ochre flame.

'Wyckedness, suche wounds,' he mutters, his eyes flashing. 'But they can be salved fer a payement.'

The doctor will treat you, but you must pay for his healing services. If you were stung by the nettles, you must pay one silver coin. If you have been hit by a shard of glass you must pay one copper coin. If you require both treatments, you must pay for both. When you have paid the doctor, turn to **194**.

250

The Arch Warlock shuffles over to one of the darkened windows. Lightning flashes in the garden. Through the trees is a view which catches your breath: the city of Suidemor. Lights twinkle from tall, spired buildings and domed roofs glow like candles under a shroud of rain. The city of the Faery.

'Suidemor be home to many fey, but it be ruled by nun,' the Warlock explains. 'There be those of great power, such as the witches and warlocks of my kin, whose ancestors came long ago frum the Mortal world. We be the lovers of nature, and diviners of natural laws. There be also the Elder Fey, who first built the city and are the rulers in name. Their magick be of a different kind, for they be lovers of mathema and science. Yet their power dwindles. There be no heir to take the throne, and even if the King had children, he would soon forgetten their names, for he languishes under a spell of terrible magick and power. It be so named, the Forgotten Spell.'

Your heart lurches at mention of the spell.

'I know of your quest to seek this spell,' continues the Warlock, 'and though I hold nun allegience to the Elder Fey, I am much troubled by the affairs of the city, for it is in danger of falling to the hands of evil.'

You follow the Warlock's penetrating gaze to the city beyond.

'The oobanata,' whispers the Warlock. 'They cometh every night, carried by wind and rain to wreak fear in the hearts of fey. They be the fumes of Olcrada's cauldrunn.'

The Warlock scowls.

'The King must return to end this evil, yet he must first be saved and there be but one way to save him. To break the Forgotten Spell, the exact words must be recited backwards in his presence. Alas, mæst fey believe the spell be long ago destroyed by Olcrada. Nay. There be another Warlock who kens it still.'

The Warlock chuckles grimly to himself and hobbles over to a desk in the nook of a tree. A lantern swings nearby, illuminating the muddle of parchments and books. His shadow rises and falls as he rummages amongst the clutter.

He returns bearing a set of three iron keys. The polished metal gleams in the firelight as he holds them out to you.

'I have hidden the spell for safekeeping. Goe now to the Church of the Blackrose Coven. There ye will find a door that leadeth to a secret room. This room be a portal betwixt my church and the Library of Suidemor on the other side of the city. In this room ye will finden a box of priestlie candles. Open the box twice – no more or less – before removing the candles. Inside, there shall be a ring, plainlie-looking and made of iron and bound by an Elder spell. The spell be Ironring, and the number be 91. This spell will bind and unbind the ring to reveal its true treasure, as writ upon quicksilver parchement – the words of the Forgotten Spell.'

The Warlock hands you the set of keys. You feel the charge of your quest weighing upon you as you take them, though your thoughts are suddenly cut off by a sound that chills you to the bone: a scream from the antechamber where the priest was keeping guard. The Warlock glares at the doors, his eyes aglow.

'The oobanata maye nun enter the house of Blackrose!' he bellows.

Thunder claps overhead. The trees shake. Through

the keyhole of the door, a tendril of vapour appears and curls around the handle.

'Quicken! Hide the keys!' commands the Warlock.

Make a note of the Ironring spell, its number and any other important information, and then turn to 228.

251

You utter the spell. To your delight, the pigeon floats free of the goblin's clutches. It hovers above them for a moment, then falls back into their hands with the weight of a stone. The goblins stare suspiciously at the bird. They cast their gaze about the shadowed lane. From their belts, they each remove a short-handled knife.

Will you make your presence known (turn to 48), or stay hidden in the shadows (turn to 127)?

252

Pearlie grips your wrist and shepherds you into the street. Her nails dig into your flesh as she drags you along. You glance about, noticing that the street is deathly silent but for the sound of the shop door slamming behind you. A thickness invades the air, something foreign and searching, something which fills you with a dread far worse than the breath of this foul hag who is leading you into the shadows of the lanes. As you glance behind, you see tendrils of vapour the colour of deep bruises slithering along the cobblestones like snakes, creeping up walls and into windows, sliding under doors and coiling themselves around lamp-posts.

'Dun look!' you hear Pearlie cry as she pulls you through a small doorway.

As you duck under the frame, her crone's hand catches your shirt and pulls you into the darkness.

Turn to **201**.

253

You smear some of the ointment on each eyelid. When you open your eyes, you see Cyleric smirking at you.

'Such devyces will do ye nun good to see through such a riddle,' he remarks.

You look sheepishly at the table. The answer is no more apparent than it was before.

Remember you only have enough eye ointment for

three applications. Make a note that you have used some, and return to **117** if you want to continue with the puzzle. If you cannot solve it, turn to **361**.

254

You try the key, but it does not turn. At the same time the Elemental lunges and you feel an icy breath on your back as you push on the door. You hear a ripping sound and feel yourself being yanked backwards. Talons tear into your flesh. A triumphant shriek fills the air, accompanied by your final valiant cry as you slump to the ground, the smell of your own blood and death rising about you, before a curtain of darkness is pulled over your eyes…

Turn to **332**.

255

You utter the spell as the Elemental strikes. You feel talons slice across your shoulder and a searing pain. You prepare for your death, but it does not come. The

Elemental retreats a step. Though it is not a creature of simple mind, your use of magic has caused it some doubt. How long it will last, you do not know, but it is all the time you need to dodge your death. You run, terrified, back down the lane.

Make a note that you have been struck by an Air Elemental and turn to **51**.

256

The frappella vines are highly poisonous and will leach your stamina as long as you leave the wounds untreated.

If you have any feverfew flowers or salve-all cream, you may use them and suffer no consequences. Otherwise, you must keep an eye out for a cure. Until you find a cure, you will be unable to cast any spells. If you have any other injuries to attend to, return to **165**. Otherwise, turn to **281**.

257

Pearlie closes her eyes and hums, rocking back and forth gently and at the same time removing a grubby little bag from the folds of her rags. She shakes the bag and throws the contents on the table in front of you. A collection of small, flat stones are scattered, each one with a symbol or letter inscribed on it. Pearlie inspects the stones, leaning over them and muttering.

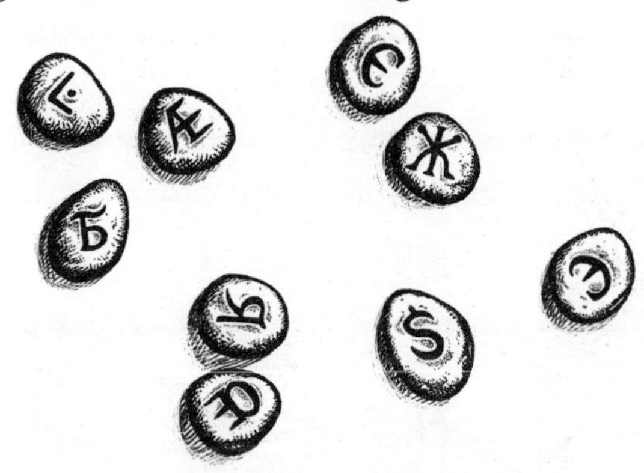

'Ai! Beware the omen of a bird, or any particulars of a bird,' Pearlie says. 'But make one allowance: be that to follow a pigeon with a broken wing.' She taps at the stones. 'B-L-A-C-K-R-O-S-E. Blackrose. Ye must find this place, but much evil awaits there for ye.'

The lamplight flickers as Pearlie stares at you, clearly frightened.

'What is Blackrose?' you ask.

Pearlie nervously scoops up the stones and puts them back in the bag.

'I know not, but I have heard of a tavern, the Blackrose Aerms. Wycked place,' she whispers. Pearlie blows out the lamp. 'Now spiruts have seen me. Ye must leave.'

Her mood has changed and there is such urgency in her words that you are compelled to gather your things and follow her out the door. You fumble up the steps in the darkness. She pushes you along the passage to the front door.

'But where is the tavern?' you ask hurriedly, as she unlocks the latch.

'Ye be the Elder Feyling. Usen yer magic!'

Pearlie prods your satchel. And with that, she pushes you out onto the street.

Turn to **60**.

258

The tram rumbles forward. You hold onto the handrails as you move along the aisle, inspecting the wares.

You may select from any of the following items, so long as you have enough coins. Turn to the numbers below to investigate your purchases. If you have any eye ointment, you may use it now by turning to **294**.

Short-bladed knife	8 coppers	turn to **308**
Miniature compass	7 coppers	turn to **40**
Shamrock ring	5 coppers	turn to **216**
Candle	3 coppers	turn to **3**
Owl-feather quill	3 coppers	turn to **183**
Bag of teeth	1 copper	turn to **203**

When you have finished making your purchases, turn to **196**.

259

You utter the spell. Even in the half light of the fallen staff, you can see that it hasn't worked. This spell is for use in the day only, and night has long ago fallen. You watch helplessly as the Warlock slumps to the floor.

Turn to **262**.

260

You try the key, but it does not work. You fumble for another key, glancing back to check the lane. To your horror, the winged shape of the Elemental is swooping low across the cobblestones. You are the prey, and this creature will be merciless. It is upon you within seconds. Deadly talons rip into your flesh. A triumphant shriek fills the air, accompanied by your final valiant cry as you slump to the ground, the smell of your own blood and death rising about you.

Turn to 332.

261

You mutter the spell. Confusion flickers across Effie's face. Your spell has made her doubtful, but that is all it has done. She licks her lips.

'Fight! Fight!' squawks the parrot in her ear.

Effie grins and pushes the table over, the only protection between you and her advance.

You scramble backwards, tripping over an upturned

chair and sprawling on the floor. Effie stands over you, a mountain of sagging flesh and foul odour. You brace yourself for her blow. Instead she lets out an enormous bellow of laughter, her broken teeth visible between mottled lips. She puckers and spits, her spittle landing just inches from you on the dirty floor. The crowd cheer. Effie dismisses you with a wave of her fat hand and lumbers over to the bar. A few other patrons spit at you for good measure as you struggle to your feet, relieved at least to be alive.

Turn to **186**.

262

A strange blue light begins to fill the chamber. It emanates from the Warlock who lies upon the floor, his body wasting before your eyes. He opens his mouth and a tendril of vapour oozes from his lips as he speaks,

'Goe! Or ye wyll nun survive, I swear this to ye!'

He shudders violently as the oobanata envelope him. His hands clutch at his robes, then suddenly go limp.

A terrible shriek fills the air. You step back from the Warlock. Rising from his body, infused with the vapours of Olcrada's cauldron, is a sinewy creature of terrifying proportions. Threads of vapour drip from its limbs like slime. Dark wings spread behind it. Black fur is stretched taut over its skeletal features, from which an icy breath escapes.

263

This creature is an Air Elemental. It is magical and highly dangerous. If you have already cast a Darkward spell, turn to **293**. If not, you may either try to cast it now, or run (turn to **187**).

263

You utter the spell as a waterhag rises from the water, her bloated skin dripping weeds and slime. She stands stupidly in the birdbath, all malice forgotten. Then slowly she begins to sink, inch by inch, back into the water. With her head just above the surface, she emits a strangled sob that evokes some pity in your heart, for the hag is surely a puppet to greater magical forces. Then she is gone. The wind drops and calm returns to the grotto. You hasten to leave.

Turn to **314**.

264

You notice a book lying on the vacated table. Sure enough, it is the Arch Warlock's book. As you pick it up, a piece of parchment flutters free of the pages. You read the scrawled words:

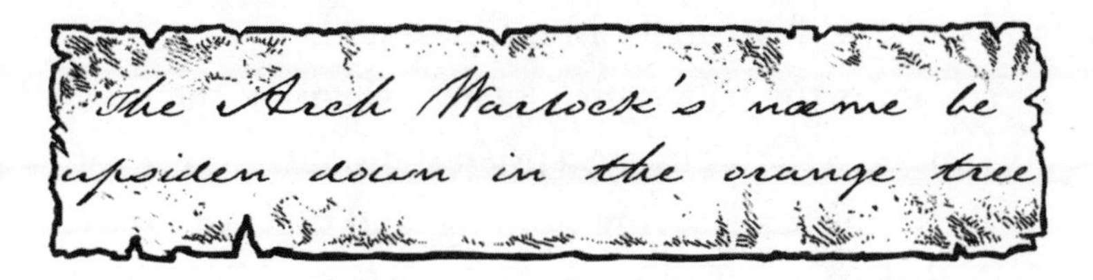

Though you don't understand the meaning of Cyleric's message, it will surely be useful. You hastily return the book to your satchel and leave the tavern.

Make a note of Cyleric's clue. Though he has stolen your possessions, you may presume that you were carrying any coins in your pockets, and therefore they are still in your possession. Make a note of your other losses and turn to **81**.

265

The dwarf grabs his glass and drinks the contents in a single swig. He belches and grins, then prods your glass towards you with his oily, unwiped fingers.

Will you join in and sip the drink (turn to **290**) or politely decline (turn to **197**)?

266

You step into a cool, damp antechamber. The floor is strangely soft underfoot, and it takes you a moment to realise that you are standing on a carpet of moss. As your eyes adjust to the dimness, you see that the room is long and wide, with an archway at the far end.

You cross the hall, your footsteps silent on the moss. As you reach the archway, a priest steps out to greet you. He bows his head, saying nothing, and leads you into a domed chamber. Tall trees grow around the walls, their branches interlocking beneath a glass ceiling. Between the trees are windows, now dark with the coming of night. The priest leaves you, closing a set of doors behind him as he goes.

'Welcome to Blackrose, friend,' speaks a voice.

You peer into the dimness but can see no one.

'Ye knoweth who I be, fer ye have openedd the door to my home,' continues the voice. 'The question be truly, who are *you*?'

You sense the speaker's gaze from the shadows, penetrating you like an icy wind.

'Blazen!' he calls.

Fire lanterns, hanging from the overhead branches, burst into flame. The chamber glows with light. A hunched figure, clothed in a cloak of green silk, stands before you. He points his staff at you. Suddenly, a flash of light flies from the tip of the staff and hits you in the chest with a power that sends you reeling backwards.

'Defend yourself!' commands the Warlock.

Can you cast any magic? If you are unable to cast spells because of injury, turn to **350**. If you have been bitten by an imp, you will also be unable to defend yourself (turn to **350**). Otherwise, you may cast a spell now.

267

As the tendrils approach, your legs grow heavy and leaden beneath you.

Do you have any vivifying elyxir (turn to **108**) or falliard bread (turn to 276)? If you have neither of these items, turn to **291**.

268

You pack away your new possessions and head back to the street.

Turn to 222.

269

Continuing on, you become aware of a pungent smell. The stench grows stronger, while up ahead you see scraps of gristle and vegetable peelings strewn over the cobblestones.

If you have been attacked by magpies, turn to **248** now. If not, turn to **86**.

270

You utter the spell as a waterhag rises from the water, her bloated skin dripping weeds and slime. She stands stupidly in the birdbath, all malice forgotten. Then slowly she begins to sink, inch by inch, back into the water. With her head just above the surface, she emits a strangled sob that evokes some pity in your heart, for the hag is surely a puppet to greater magical forces. Then she is gone. The wind drops and calm returns to the grotto. You hasten to leave.

Turn to **314**.

271

You open the box twice. Inside is a row of thick candles, which you carefully lift out. Undeneath the candles, you find two items – a black iron ring, and an envelope. Heart pounding, you seize the ring and hold it up to the candlelight. It is dull and roughly-made, neither beautiful nor valuable: the perfect disguise.

You may cast the Ironring spell now.

272

You utter the spell, praying for it to work. To your amazement, the oobanata release their stranglehold on the Warlock. The tendrils circle his body, held at bay. The Warlock gazes at you through glazed eyes.

'Ye have the power of the halven-fey, yet I fear ye have only prolonged my death. 'Tis time enough for this last piece of telling: though there be three keys, there be only one door. Goe!'

With these words, the Warlock slumps to the floor.

Turn to 262.

273

You utter the spell under your breath. The goblins look very much awake despite your spell. They toss the pigeon in the air and you realise from the dead weight of the bird that you have sent the pigeon to sleep instead! The goblins stare suspiciously at the bird. They cast their gaze about the shadowed lane. From their belts, they each remove a short-handled knife.

Will you make your presence known (turn to 48), or stay hidden in the shadows (turn to 127)?

274

This spell is a preventative spell. It will stop the goblin casting another spell on you, but it will not revoke the magic already cast.

Turn to 283.

275

A breath of cold air greets you as you step down from the tram. You are standing at the end of the tramline. Steam and smoke fill the air as the tram reverses on its tracks and begins its journey back to the city. Soon you are alone, standing before a ten-foot wall of stone. You approach the wall and examine it carefully. There is no entrance to speak of, but there is an engraving on one of the stones, which reads:

Blackrose
The Coven of the
Arch Warlock of Suidemor

Welcome, friend

Do you want to try knocking (turn to **348**), try climbing the wall (turn to **301**) or cast a spell?

276

You reach into your satchel and find the falliard bread. You eat it as fast as you can, willing your throat to swallow even as your breath constricts in the deadly air. Feeling returns to your legs. You turn and run.

Make a note that you have used the falliard bread, and turn to **163**.

277

A quick glance around the tavern tells you that Cyleric is gone. There is nothing you can do to retrieve your things. Cursing your misfortune, you hastily leave the tavern.

You may presume that you were carrying any coins in your pockets, and therefore they are still in your possession. Make a note of your other losses and turn to **81**.

278

You mumble that the paper is blank and there is nothing to read. Pearlie glares at you.

'Cræfty halven! I be living fer 400 years! Pearlie saw it. Pearlie catch it. Pearlie sæve yer life!'

She is clearly upset at your lack of trust. She snatches your spellbook.

'If ye know nun of the message, then ye will nun be needed of this,' she says. 'Pearlie will keepen it, as payement fer her givings.'

You cannot do without your spellbook. You have no choice but to bribe it back by offering to read the note. You must also offer her one other bribe from your satchel, be it food, coin, herb or medicine. Make a note of your loss and turn to **236**.

279

You approach the door and gently push down on the old iron handle. To your surprise, it turns. You pull the door open and step into a narrow lane enclosed by an arbour of overhanging vines. The stems are covered in broad green leaves and pendulous yellow flowers. Insects buzz in the warm air and birds twitter in the branches overhead.

These vines are frapella vines. If the priest gave you any advice, you can follow it now. Otherwise, you can follow the path under the arbour (turn to 204), look for a way around it (turn to 225) or go back the way you came (turn to 182).

280

You offer the imp a trade from your possessions. The creature clutches the tin possessively and indicates that he wants everything in your satchel.

If you have enough possessions, you may give the imp no less than three items (including coins, if you prefer), in exchange for the powder. If not, you will have to choose something else (return to 211). If you still need to choose a second item, you may also return to 211. If you have finished choosing your items, turn to 173.

281

You begin to follow the path towards the building. As you pass the statues you notice with some unease that

the faces all seem to be carved into tortured and frightened expressions. You hurry on. At the entrance to the building, a pair of stone trolls with grimacing expressions stand like guards on either side of a door. Candles are posted around the door frame, protected under lanterns of golden-stained glass. The candlelight illuminates a great work of art impressed on the main panel of the door. It is an enormous painting depicting a tree framed by black bramble roses. You gaze at it in wonder. Words have been laid in tile along the bottom of the painting. They read:

SPEAKE THE NAME OF HE WHO DWELLETH
SPEAKE IT ONCE, OR ELSE BEWARE
TO STONE BE TURNEDD, UNLESS YE CARETH
TO FYND THE NAME AS WRITTEN HERE

You consider the message, a chill running through you. The statues are fey that have been turned to stone. Which name did they speak? And which name will *you* speak?

Examine the mosaic picture on the facing page. Hidden somewhere in the picture is the name of the Arch Warlock. You will have to study it very carefully, as there have been many who have gone before you and failed. Once you have found the name, turn to **334**. If you have some eye ointment and you would like to use it to help you, turn to **306**. If you cannot find the name, turn to **365**.

282

You ask the dwarf if he has heard of the Forgotten Spell. He gawps at you, then breaks out in sputtering laughter. He bellows to a fellow dwarf sitting at a nearby table.

'This feyling be looking fer the Forgotten Spell. Have ye seen it, friend?'

Laughter breaks out around you. You glance about, alarmed at the attention you are beginning to draw. Clearly, the dwarf has no information for you.

You may leave the table and try sitting next to the troll (turn to **343**) or the drunk (turn to **208**).

283

You stand helpless before the goblin. Behind him, a host of onlookers watch your fate.

'Where be me purse, feyling?' he asks menacingly.

At the same time you hear a shriek from the passengers.

'Imp! Imp!' screams a faerie, flapping her wings and flying up to the ceiling.

Confusion breaks out as passengers start leaping about.

'Eeech!' cries the goblin, jumping in the air.

With the distraction, you feel the spell loosening. Ignoring the chaos in the tram, you begin to move your limbs slowly, wading towards the door as if through gooey syrup. As the tram slows down, you push open the door and swing to the ground, landing hard on the street as your legs buckle under you.

You will have to undo this spell quickly! You now have time to search through your spellbook for the right spell.

284

It has taken you all night to find the books. You are covered in cobwebs and dust, and in need of warmth and a solid meal. You hurriedly leave the room, carrying all three books.

If you were stung by the nettles in the prison, turn to 67. If not, turn to 198.

285

The dwarf watches you, sneering, as you mutter the spell. Nothing happens. Sniggering laughs and whispering can be heard in the gathered crowd.

'Begone ye, feyling! Bring me some true amusement!' hollers the dwarf.

You see you have been discredited. With as much dignity as you can muster, you push your chair back and slip into the crowd, ignoring the jeers behind you.

Turn to **186**.

286

You study the bowls, but can see no pattern. You will have to dice with death and guess which order they are in.

Choose between the following sequences:

123 132 213 231 312 321

If you have a shamrock, turn instead to **355**.

287

You mutter the spell quickly and your limbs loosen immediately. You push open the tram door and jump into the street, ignoring the jeers from the passengers.

Turn to 167.

288

You utter the spell. The words on the plaque change before your eyes to read:

The door be unlocked,
friend

What door? The stone wall is solid under your hand, just as it appears to your eye. You inspect it from top to bottom, but can find no magical entrance. You step back, hoping a broader view might reveal the secret, when suddenly you trip on something. You look down to see an iron handle set in the cobblestones.

Excited, you grasp the handle and pull hard. A square area of stones lifts away from the pavement as the door opens. Looking down, you see torchlit, spiral steps leading into the darkness.

Turn to **336**.

289

Remembering the priest's advice, you begin to sing softly as you walk under the arbour. It is strangely pleasant here, with the ground spongy underfoot and the perfume of flowers wafting in the air. You carry on singing, following the small path as it curves around and leads at length to another door.

Turn to **214**.

290

The liquid is warm and smells spicy and good. You take a sip. To your surprise, the drink tastes wonderful.

'The wine of all sorrows. Smooth as a wood nymph's cheek, but dangerous nevertheless,' says the dwarf with a wink, as you quickly finish it.

As you place the glass on the table, your head feels suddenly foggy. You realise that this faery potion is very alcoholic. The sounds of the tavern merge into a single throbbing noise that fills your head. You see the dwarf speaking to you, but you cannot hear the words. Colour seems to drain from the world. You clutch at the table to steady yourself, but your fingers slip off the wood as you fall to the floor.

If you have a bottle of vivifying elixir, turn to **114**. If not, turn to 22.

291

As much as you will your legs to move, it is no use against the oobanata, the vapour from Olcrada's cauldrons. You are in his territory and your escape from his prison has unleashed his wrath. You watch helplessly as the vapour glides across the cobblestones towards you. Your knees buckle and you sink to the ground. As the vapour touches your skin, it coils around your limbs and you feel your breath being sucked from you. You collapse into blackness…

Turn to **368**.

292

You light your candle by blowing on the wick. The small glow lights the path between the brambles. You make your way into the dark, listening for sounds of life or danger, but all you hear is your own heart hammering in your chest. The pathway soon begins to slope upwards, and you can make out a sliver of light that marks the exit. You hurry on as fast as you can, keen to be free of the tunnel.

Turn to **165**.

293

The creature shrieks and beats its wings, rising into the air and hovering before you, a dense body of energy held in check only by the thin veneer of your elementary spell. '*The church …*,' the Warlock had said. Without hesitation, you turn and run.

Turn to **303**.

294

You smear the ointment on each eyelid. When you open your eyes, you see that some of the wares on display are not what they seem. The knife is quite rusty and not worth eight coppers, though it might be useful if you need to defend yourself with a weapon. If you wish to purchase it, you may haggle with the vendor and pay only four coppers. The ring is made of tin and you may purchase it for only two coppers. The owl feather is cursed. The bag of teeth may be turned into more coppers, while the compass and candle seem to be authentic.

Return to 258 to make any purchases.

295

You utter the spell, praying for it to work. To your amazement, the oobanata release their stranglehold on the Warlock. The tendrils circle his body, held at bay. The Warlock gazes at you through glazed eyes.

'Ye have the power of the halven-fey, yet I fear ye have only prolonged my death. 'Tis time enough for this last piece of telling: though there be three keys, there be only one door. Now goe!'

With these words, the Warlock slumps to the floor.

Turn to 262.

296

You mutter the spell. Effie staggers suddenly, losing her balance and crashing into the table. The parrot squawks and the onlookers cheer as the table cracks under her weight. Your spell has knocked her down, but that is all it has done. You watch in alarm as Effie gets to her feet, shaking herself to her senses.

'Fight! Fight!' squawks the parrot in her ear.

Effie grins and pushes the table wreckage aside, the only protection between you and her advance.

You scramble backwards, tripping over an upturned

chair and sprawling on the floor. Effie stands over you, a mountain of sagging flesh and foul odour. You brace yourself for her blow. Instead she lets out an enormous bellow of laughter, her broken teeth visible between mottled lips. She puckers and spits at you. The crowd cheer. Effie dismisses you with a wave of her fat hand and lumbers over to the bar. A few patrons spit at you for good measure as you struggle to your feet, relieved at least to be alive.

Turn to **186**.

297

You mutter the spell quickly. The Warlock's voice booms out across the chamber.

'Ye have much to learn. That spell be only for daye. Twilight has passed and the nyght has now come.'

He points at the night beyond the windows, mocking

you. You try to stand up, but you realise that you have no control over your limbs. The Warlock chants the curse:

Slymedd blod like myre
Weter upon fyre
Mudden, sond, brickle, quire
Meken slough and tire

Your limbs become impossibly heavy. Your tongue feels thick and useless, and as you try to draw in breath, your throat constricts. You gasp for air, clutching helplessly at the floor. You are completely within the Warlock's power.

Turn to **350**.

298

The dwarf watches you, sneering, as you focus on the empty plate of bones and mutter the spell. The bones begin to shake of their own accord. Onlookers murmur their approval. The dwarf drums his hands on the table, adding to the atmosphere, but breaking your concentration. The plate bounces in the air as he lifts the table clean up with his strong hands. The crowd cheer as the plate flies through the air and lands with a smash. The dwarf breaks into a broad grin. Although you were sure your spell was working, if only for a moment, he is passing it off as a joke.

'Begone ye, feyling,' he leers at you.

You see you have been discredited. With as much dignity as you can muster, you push your chair back and slip into the crowd, ignoring the jeers behind you.

Turn to **186**.

299

You stand discreetly against the wall as the tram grinds forward. Avoiding the gaze of the other passengers, you inspect a scrawl of graffiti on the wall.

You have the Elder Fey sight. Perhaps you can see the hidden number in the graffiti, as shown in the picture above? Keep a note of this paragraph number, then turn to the hidden number if you find it.

The tram emits a belch of steam. An official-looking faery in a conductor's uniform comes striding through the carriage, kicking a chicken out of his way as he goes.

'Blackrose! End of the line! Blackrose!'

A subdued murmur ripples through the carriage. Passengers glance nervously out of the windows. This part of the city is eerily deserted. High, stone walls line the pavements, strangled by weeds and winter-bare vines. The sky darkens under a gauze of grey cloud.

The conductor gawps at you as you pull the bell, clearly not expecting anyone to disembark.

'No good witcherie,' he mutters as he reluctantly opens the door.

A breath of cold air greets you as you step down from the tram.

Turn to 275.

300

You inch back towards the door. Each footstep seems to echo loudly, and in your nervousness, you stumble over the monk's staff. You freeze. There, in the shadows at the top of the staircase, you see a shape shifting in its hiding place and the gleam of maniacal, merciless eyes

looking down upon you. Blood pounds through your body and the Darkward spell slips from your command. In desperation, you snatch up the monk's staff and grip the handle with sweating hands. Though it didn't save the monk, it might well save you.

An ear-splitting shriek fills the chamber, the sound reverberating off the surfaces like splintered glass. The Elemental launches itself from the staircase and swoops down on you with wings spread like a sorcerer's cape. You duck, at the same time swinging the staff like a club as hard as you can. The staff hits the hind leg of the creature, throwing it off balance. You raise the staff a second time, wielding it blindly and connecting with the clawed foot of the Elemental. There is a terrible crunching sound as bones shatter. The creature shrieks again, this time from pain. You scramble away from it and run to the door. Reaching the sanctuary of the wooden panels, you are relieved to find the symbol of the rose, inscribed into the wood. You fumble for the right key, your hands shaking, fatigue fraying at the edges of your mind. There is only one way for you to go now.

Check the rose insignia on the door and match it to a key.

301

You hoist yourself up the jutting stonework. The climb is easy enough and you are soon within reach of the top, but as you stretch out for the final stones, your hand touches something extremely cold and slimey. Your fingers slip and you tumble backwards, landing heavily on the cobblestones below.

You lie for a moment on the ground, your body wracked with various pains. The cold wind stings your face and eventually you force yourself to move. You test each one of your limbs slowly, but nothing seems to be broken except your pride. You stand up, a little shakily, and face the wall once more. Looking up, you can now see the layer of deadly slime that covers the top of the wall. Such a simple security device, yet so effective!

Will you try knocking now (turn to **348**), or do you want to cast a spell?

302

You walk some distance, proceeding slowly as you try to find a path through the brambles. At last you see the end of the lane. It appears to come to a dead end, though as you draw close, you notice the indistinct shape of a door, hidden behind the rose brambles.

Would you like to try the door (turn to **279**), or go back to the junction and try the other direction (turn to **195**)?

303

You run blindly back through the antechamber, tripping over an obstacle near the doorway. You realise that you have tripped over the dead priest. You scramble to your feet and open the heavy door, stepping outside into the lashing rain and wind, pulling the door shut behind you.

You may cast a locking spell now, or run for cover (turn to **146**).

304

You mutter the spell quickly. The Warlock's voice booms out across the chamber.

'Ye have much to learn, fer I be a magickal fey, and that spell be cast only upon dogs and mice and fey of symple mind. Perhaps ye be of symple mind also?'

The Warlock is mocking you. You try to stand up, but you realise that you have no control over your limbs. The Warlock chants the curse:

Slymedd blod like myre
Weter upon fyre
Mudden, sond, brickle, quire
Meken slough and tire

Your limbs become impossibly heavy. Your tongue feels thick and useless, and as you try to draw in breath, your throat constricts. You gasp for air, clutching helplessly at the floor. You are completely within the Warlock's power.

Turn to **350**.

305

You utter the spell as the waterhag rises from the water, her bloated skin dripping weeds and slime. She steps from the birdbath, her great feet flattening the ferns, then sways and suddenly collapses into the pool. Water splashes up and the smell of rotten slime reaches your nose. As the hag sinks under the water, she evokes some pity in your heart, for she is surely a puppet to greater magical forces. Then she is gone. The wind drops and calm returns to the grotto. You hasten to leave.

Turn to **314**.

306

You smear some of the ointment on your eyelids. When you open them, the name becomes immediately apparent – it is upside-down in the orange tree!

Return to **281** and turn the picture upside-down to reveal the answer.

307

The shamrock has been pressed and preserved in a hard, thin resin. You hope it will bestow more luck on you than it did on its previous owner.

Return to your previous paragraph.

308

The knife is serviceable enough, though not worth the eight coppers you paid for it. Nonetheless, it may prove useful should you need to defend yourself with a weapon.

Return to 258.

309

You open the box. Inside is a row of thick candles. As you lift the candles out, a cloud of sweet-scented vapour is released. Otherwise, the box is empty. You realise too late that you have activated a trap. This alcove will become your coffin after all, as you breathe in the deadly fumes of the Lonely Moor Mist. The keys fall from your hand as you collapse to the floor…

Turn to 368.

310

You give the gate a wide berth, ignoring the pleas from the young girl. Leaving the orange tree behind, you follow the lane until the path begins to slope downwards, eventually coming to a set of stairs that leads into a tunnel, overgrown and choked with dead brambles.

Navigating the tunnel in the dark will be dangerous. Do you have a candle? If you do, turn to 292. If not, turn to 141.

311

You carve your triangle. Effie's beady eyes flash excitedly. She carves a cross in the centre of the squares, then leans back with folded fleshy arms to watch. You see immediately that you have made a big mistake.

Turn to 26.

312

Hoping you have the correct order for the bowls, you sup from the ones you think you need. The Warlock watches you grimly. Your attempt to guess was as brave as it was doomed. You feel a sudden stab of pain in your stomach. You cry out, doubling over on the mossy floor as the pain stabs again.

'Fool ye nun with the powers of Witcherie,' intones the Arch Warlock, 'fer death be the penance.'

Sure enough, as the pain wracks your body, your vision fails and you fall into darkness…

Turn to **368**.

313

You carve your triangle roughly in the wood. Effie examines your move and carves a cross in reply.

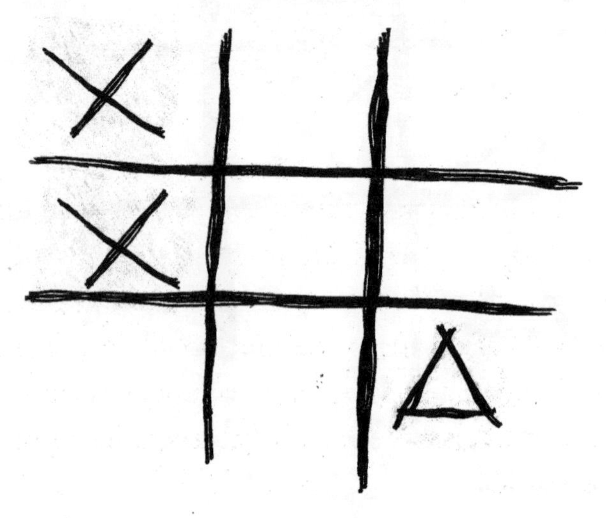

There is only one move you can make to stop her from getting three crosses in a row.

Turn to **205**.

314

You return to the junction and turn right. This lane is much the same as the last. Continuing on, you become aware of a pungent smell. The stench grows stronger, while up ahead you see scraps of gristle and vegetable peelings strewn over the cobblestones.

If you have been attacked by birds, turn to **248** now. If not, turn to **86**.

315

You insert the key and turn it as the Elemental lunges. You feel an icy breath on your back, followed by a ripping sound as the talons tear into your satchel. You are yanked backwards by the straps. You twist free, leaving the Elemental to its spoils as you open the door and stumble through, heedless of what might lie beyond.

Turn to **157**.

316

You make your way across the chamber towards the staircase. Each footstep seems to echo loudly. As you reach the staircase, you look up. There, in the shadows at the top of the staircase, you see a shape shifting in its hiding place and the gleam of maniacal, merciless eyes looking down upon you. You freeze. Blood pounds through your body. The creature's shriek fills the chamber, the sound reverberating off the surfaces like splintered glass. It launches itself from the staircase and swoops down on you with wings spread. The Elemental is upon you within seconds. Deadly talons tear into your flesh. You slump to the ground, the smell of your own blood and death rising about you.

Turn to **332**.

317

You may speak the Warlock's name if you dare.

To speak the name, transcribe each letter into a number using the faery alphabet at the back of your spellbook. Add the numbers together, then turn to the answer. If the page does not make sense, turn to **301**.

318

Following the lane, you walk some distance. The air is still and close. You come at length to a junction. Looking left, then right, you find no signs to indicate which way to go.

You will have to rely on luck and intuition to navigate this maze. Would you like to go left (turn to **244**), or right (turn to **65**)?

319

You hastily check the compass needle. It quivers towards the right.

Turn to **155**.

320

The dwarf watches you, sneering, as you mutter the spell. His eyelids slowly sag and his head drops to his chest. Onlookers murmur their approval at the sound of his snores. A cheer erupts. Then the dwarf suddenly snaps his head up, wide awake, and breaks into a broad grin. Although you are sure your spell worked, if only for a moment, he is passing it off as a joke.

'Begone ye, feyling,' he leers at you.

You see you have been discredited. With as much dignity as you can muster, you push your chair back and slip into the crowd, ignoring the jeers behind you.

Turn to **186**.

321

Hoping you have the correct order for the bowls, you sup from the ones you think you need. The Warlock watches you grimly. Your attempt to guess was as brave as it was doomed. You feel a sudden stab of pain in your stomach. You cry out, doubling over on the mossy floor as the pain stabs again.

'Fool ye nun with the powers of Witcherie,' intones the Arch Warlock, 'fer death be the penance.'

Sure enough, as the pain wracks your body, your vision fails and you fall into darkness...

Turn to **368**.

322

You insert the key. The tumblers click and you yank the door open.

Turn to 97.

323

You hurry back to the junction, aware of the darkening sky.

You may turn left (turn to **90**), or continue straight ahead (turn to **244**).

324

The key turns in the lock. You push the door open and tumble inside. Glancing back, you see the winged shape of the Elemental swooping low across the cobblestones. A merciless shriek fills the night air. You fumble for the bolt, pushing the door shut and locking it behind you just as the Elemental crashes into it, talons tearing at the wood.

You gasp for breath, safe for the moment. The church is in darkness, save for a few candles still burning around the walls. You grab one of these candles from its holder and step into the main chamber. On the floor in front of you lies a pile of robes and the monk's staff. The robes are of cream material embroidered with black roses. They are smouldering, burnt in places, and empty. A chill runs through you. The monk is surely dead. Where then is his body? Like the Warlock, did an Air Elemental rise from his corpse?

You scan the darkened corners of the chamber for signs of movement. Pictures have been ripped from the walls, windows broken. Lingering in the air is the scent of incense and of something else – the bitter smell of death. You ponder the Warlock's words: '*In the Church of the Blackrose Coven, there be a door that leadeth to a secret room...*' Where? You can see no other doors. Surely the door by which you entered will lead back into the lane? Not a comforting thought, considering the creature that awaits you. Or you could try climbing the stairs that lead to the street. Yet the staircase may entrap you, making you fair game for the second Elemental that almost certainly lies in wait for you.

Which will you choose? If you would like to try the staircase door, turn to **316**. If you would like to investigate the lane door, turn to **300**.

325

You carve your triangle. Effie's beady eyes flash excitedly. She carves a cross in the centre of the squares, then leans back with folded, fleshy arms to watch. You see immediately that you have made a big mistake.

Turn to 26.

326

With the imp gone, you investigate the purse. Inside the folds of leather, you find several items.

Keep a note of this paragraph number in order to return to it after investigating each item. You may keep as many items as you like.

Silver coins (turn to 349).

A box of matches (turn to 12).

A pressed shamrock (turn to 307).

A tin of snuff (turn to 352).

When you have finished, turn to 268.

327

You mutter the spell and your limbs loosen immediately. You run from the tram, ignoring the jeers from the passengers.

Turn to **167**.

328

You hurry through the tunnel, your hands soon scratched as you find a path forward in the dark. An icy wind roars down the tunnel behind you. You look back to see bramble branches being ripped from the walls and the shape of the Elemental advancing through the swirling debris. Heedless of the thorns, you escape at last into the lanes. Rain assaults you as you break into a run, your boots slipping on the wet cobblestones and splashing in puddles between them. You run blindly, your breathing ragged and low.

You are in danger of becoming cornered in the labyrinth. Do you have a compass? If you do, turn now to

319. If not, you will have to rely on luck and intuition. Choose between the following routes:

Route 1: **155**.
Route 2: **356**.
Route 3: **338**.

Or, if you have a shamrock, you may turn to **360** instead.

329

You utter the spell. The creature shrieks and beats its wings, rising into the air and hovering before you, a dense body of energy held in check only by the thin veneer of your elementary spell. '*The church* ...,' the Warlock had said. Without hesitation, you turn and run.

Turn to **303**.

330

You stand discreetly against the wall as the tram grinds forward. Avoiding the gaze of the other passengers, you inspect a scrawl of graffiti on the wall.

You have the Elder Fey sight. Perhaps you can see the hidden number in the graffiti, as shown in the picture above? Keep a note of this paragraph number, then turn to the hidden number if you can find it.

As you study the wall, you become aware of someone watching you. You turn to catch the gaze of a merchant faery weaving his way through the crowded tram. As he comes upon you, he opens his cloak with a theatrical sweep, revealing pocketfuls of crafted candles held within. He points at each candle with a practised finger.

'Spoolwax, besin, cottonseed, lutin-earwax – very rare, goodlie price – and this one, symplie beeswax; mind, wyth magic.'

He holds aloft the beeswax candle and blows expertly on the wick. A small flame ignites.

'Spare four coppers fer this one,' says the merchant with a wink.

If you do not wish to purchase the candle, turn to **33**. If you would like to purchase the candle, you may need to enchant some geld. You may use any of the following items to create four coppers:

Toffee apples
Geldwort seeds

Cast the geld spell now, if you have one of these items. Alternatively, you may offer the merchant whatever geld you currently possess (turn to **358**).

331

You continue down the lane, soon arriving at another junction. The lanes appear identical, each one thick with brambles.

You may turn either right (turn to **302**) or left (turn to **195**).

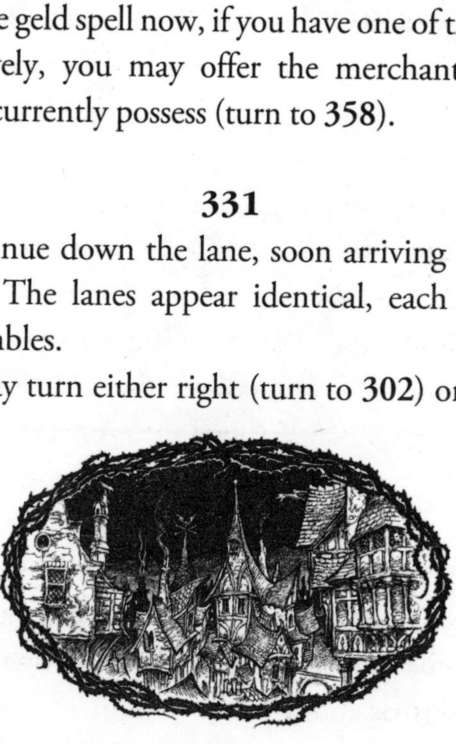

332

Death by an Elemental is painful (as you would expect), but unusual in one regard: it is remarkably slow. The poison from the creature's talons serves to render the victim unconscious. The victim is then taken back to the Elemental's lair, where the creature prays on the life force of the body over a period of many years.

Disgusting as this sounds, it is advantageous to you, as there is time enough for you to invoke one of the gifts of the Elder Fey: the power of restoration that is the birthright of all Elder Fey.

If you have already invoked these powers during your adventure, you may follow the instructions as before on **368**. If not, turn to **368** again to find out about your powers.

333

You utter the spell. The Warlock suddenly gasps and drops his staff. Where it lands the moss is singed and a trail of smoke rises – the staff is glowing hot! The Warlock regards you with admiration.

''Tis a powerful caster who can use such a spell upon a warlock with any effect,' he says. He utters a word and his staff is returned to his hand. ''Tis time, then, to tell ye of greater affairs, and to help ye with yer quest.'

Turn to **250**.

334

You may speak the Warlock's name if you dare.

To speak the name, transcribe each letter into a number using the faery alphabet at the back of your spellbook. Add the numbers together, then turn to the answer.

335

You utter the spell and a desperate prayer for it to work. The iron latch clicks in place. You check the door – it is firmly locked. For how long, you do not know, but you may have at least bought some time. You dash across the courtyard, following the statue-lined pathway. You arrive at the tunnel entrance and squeeze through the brambles.

The bramble thorns are magical and will not poison you so long as you are protected by the Darkward spell.

Turn to 328.

336

You make your way down the stairs, closing the trap-door behind you. As you decend, a light from below illuminates a patterned tile floor. The sweet smell of burning incense reaches your nose. Reaching the bottom, you find yourself standing in a magnificent hall. High windows allow the light of the darkening sky to enter. Candles flicker around the walls, revealing strange symbols etched into wood. Otherwise the room is dim. At one end of the hall, steps lead upwards to a large, ornamental door.

'Welcome to Blackrose,' a voice says from the shadows.

You spin around and lay eyes on an elderly priest, seated at a table spread with parchments. He rises slowly and steps into the light of the hall, revealing himself to be small and wizened, wearing a cream robe embroidered with black roses.

'What seeketh ye at our Coven?' he asks, regarding you with watery eyes.

You tell him you wish to see the Arch Warlock. The old priest is silent for a moment, his breath wheezing in and out.

'Did ye bringen any gift for the Warlock?' he asks.

Do you have a book to give the Warlock? If so, turn to the number on the front of the book now. If you do not, turn to **347**.

337

There is only one way to go and that is back the way you came. You dash down the lane, heart hammering in your chest. Behind you are the murderous wails of the banshee woman. She does not, however, appear to be chasing you, and at last you stop running.

You gasp for breath, shaken by your encounter but otherwise unharmed. After a time you gather your reserves of courage and begin following your new direction in earnest. Though you have escaped the banshee, you dread to think what other creatures may be waiting for you in the lanes of the Blackrose Coven.

Turn to **318**.

338

You follow the lane to the right, moving quickly in the darkness. Your cloak and boots are soon soaked through with rain. Behind you, the howling wind wreaks a path of destruction, snapping branches and tearing brambles from their roots. The Air Elemental is close on your heels. You run into a narrow lane and slide to a halt on the wet cobblestones. Standing in the middle of the lane is a mangy dog, its teeth bared and jaws salivating. It leaps past you, lunging at the Elemental that swoops behind you in attack. The dog's yowl fills the air. Leaning breathlessly against the wall, you watch as the beast is skewered to its death. With the Elemental momentarily distracted, you quickly scramble to your feet and run, terrified, down the lane.

Turn to **51**.

339

You mutter the spell quickly. The Warlock's voice booms out across the chamber.

'Ye have much to learn, fer I be a magickal fey, and that spell be cast only upon dogs, mice or fey of symple mind. Perhaps ye be of symple mind also?'

The Warlock is mocking you. You try to stand up, but you realise that you have no control over your limbs. The Warlock chants the curse:

Slymedd blod like myre
Weter upon fyre
Mudden, sond, brickle, quire
Meken slough and tire

Your limbs become impossibly heavy. Your tongue feels thick and useless, and as you try to draw in breath, your throat constricts. You gasp for air, clutching helplessly at the floor. You are completely within the Warlock's power.

Turn to **350**.

340

You follow the pigeon into a labyrinth of lanes. Towering buildings block the light, keeping the air cold and damp. Your boots splash in puddles of melted snow as you hurry on. At last you arrive in a dingy lane crowded with shops and traders. Twisted trees grow between the buildings, their branches bearing shop signs hung from chains or nails. You cast your eye across the scene in time to see the pigeon come to rest outside the door of a grime-windowed tavern across the road.

You approach the tavern. A wooden sign above the door proclaims you to be at:

THE BRACKENROSE ARMS

You gaze at the sign in excitement. Pearlie had said the Blackrose Arms, you are sure, but the pigeon has led you here. It could hardly be a coincidence. Your thoughts are interrupted by the sound of soft cooing. You look down to see the pigeon, trembling in the gutter.

Do you have a bannoch biscuit (turn to 17) or salve-all cream (turn to 2)? If you have neither of these items, then there is nothing you can do for the pigeon and you must enter the tavern instead (turn to 168).

341

You utter the spell. The words on the plaque change before your eyes to read:

The door be unlocked, friend

What door? The stone wall is solid under your hand, just as it appears to your eye. You inspect it from top to bottom, but can find no magical entrance. You step back, hoping a broader view might reveal the secret, when suddenly you trip on something. You look down to see an iron handle set in the cobblestones.

Excited, you grasp the handle and pull hard. A square area of stones lifts away from the pavement as the door opens. Looking down, you see a set of torchlit, spiral steps leading into the darkness.

Turn to 336.

342

You scramble up the wall, using the stones for purchase. But as you near the top, you find the stones are covered in a cold, slimy substance. You panic as you try in vain to grip them. Your fingers slip and you fall backwards, landing hard on the ground. The Elemental towers over you, snorting at the rain and blowing out steamy breath. Up close, you can smell the Elemental's sweating body and matted fur, intermingled wirh the smell of your own fear. You feel the Darkward spell slipping from your command.

Do you have a knife? If so, turn to **130**. If not, turn to **199**.

343

You approach the troll at the table. You see that it is a female troll, her rough features set in a wide expanse of mottled skin and framed by a mane of matted hair. On her shoulder is a striking parrot with a red belly. The parrot gawps at you, but the troll's attention is transfixed by the performance at the bar. You hesitate, then take a seat at the other end of the table.

No sooner have you sat down than the parrot lets out an enormous squawk. The sound is enough to turn every head in the tavern. You glance about nervously, meeting the hard stares of the patrons. You could not be more conspicuous! The troll turns to regard you, the folds of skin around her enormous neck shifting like sacks of sand. She brings a fat, flat hand down on the table in front of you.

'Effie's table!' she pronounces.

With the other hand she brings a short-bladed knife to a quivering halt in the woodwork.

'Naught and crosse!' she says.

The parrot jumps up and down on her shoulder. 'Naught and crosse!' it squawks. You look down at the table to see the etched lines of what appear to be many previous games of noughts and crosses. Effie is challenging you.

Do you want to accept Effie's challenge (turn to **366**) or refuse the challenge and leave the table (turn to **223**)?

344

You try the key, but it does not turn. At the same time the Elemental lunges and you feel an icy breath on your back as you push on the door. You hear a ripping sound and feel yourself being yanked backwards. Talons tear into your flesh. A triumphant shriek fills the air, accompanied by your final valiant cry as you slump to the ground, the smell of your own blood and death rising about you, before a curtain of darkness is pulled over your eyes…

Turn to 332.

345

Embarrassed by the turn of events, you alight from the tram at the next stop. You ignore the jeers from the windows as the machine rumbles past.

Turn to 222.

346

Your shoulder is throbbing painfully and you can no longer ignore it.

If you have any feverfew flowers or salve-all cream, you may use them now to treat your injuries and suffer no consequences. Otherwise, you must keep an eye out for a cure. Until you find a cure, you will be unable to cast any spells.

If you have any other injuries to attend to, return to 165. Otherwise, turn to 281.

347

You tell the priest you have nothing for the Warlock. He nods.

'It matters nun. The path to the Arch Warlock be always opened to those who be strong of heart.'

He gestures towards the door at the top of the steps.

'Though it be protected by many devyces to fool the wycked. Ye may see how ye fare.'

You gaze at the door. It is twice your height at least, held shut by an iron latch. At the priest's invitation, you climb the worn steps and pull the latch.

Turn to 83.

348

You knock on the plaque. The words change before your eyes to read:

The door be open,
friend

What door? The stone wall is solid under your hand, just as it appears to your eye. You inspect it from top to bottom, but can find no magical entrance. You step back, hoping a broader view might reveal the secret, when suddenly you trip on something. You look down to see an iron handle set in the cobblestones.

Excited, you grasp the handle and pull hard. A square area of stones lifts away from the pavement as the door opens. Looking down, you see a set of torchlit, spiral steps leading into the darkness.

Turn to **336**.

349

There are four silver coins. They appear to be genuine.

Return to your previous paragraph.

350

Without magic, you are powerless against the Warlock's spells.

'Perhaps ye have only the luck of a fool to survive this long in Suidemor,' he says. 'To lose yer magick cræft is indeed foolish. That be as it maye, I shalle offer a chance to ye.'

With these words he releases the spell. You get to your feet, gasping for breath. The Warlock points his staff at a round table in the middle of the room. Sitting on the polished wood are three bowls, each containing a steaming broth.

'Take ye now of the medicinnes ye require,' he says. He then begins to chant:

One be for wounds, lesions and bites
Two be for poisons, fevers and frights
Three be for curses, malice or spite

'Ye must sup only frum the bowls of yer need, though they be nun in order,' continues the Warlock. 'If ye sup otherwise, ye will be rightlie poisoned.'

Examine the patterns on the sides of the bowls. Can you work out which bowl is number one, number two and number three? Write down the number of the bowl underneath, then turn to the three-digit number that appears. If you cannot work out which bowls are which, turn to **286**.

351

You open the box. Inside is a row of thick candles. You close the box again, open it, close it and open it for the third time. Heart pounding, you carefully lift out the candles. The box is empty, save for a cloud of sweet-scented vapour that is released. You realise too late that you have activated a trap. This alcove will become your coffin after all, as you breathe in the deadly fumes of the Lonely Moor Mist. The keys fall from your hand as you collapse to the floor…

Turn to **368**.

352

The tin is made of sturdy metal. Inside is a ground tobacco of a deep yellow colour. You can see no immediate use for it, though it is light enough to carry should you want to keep it.

Return to your previous paragraph.

353

The banshee woman turns on you, her face glowing. Pointing her finger, she laughs and utters a string of unintelligible words. Pain flares in your throat, as though someone has sunk a knife into your neck. The banshee woman screams again and floats off down the lane, arms flailing. You clutch at your neck, feeling the skin intact. The pain quickly subsides, but when you try to cough, a hoarse whispering sound is all that you can make.

The banshee woman has cursed you as a whispering mute. You may speak, but you will be unable to cast any spells without the full power of your voice. Until you find a cure, you will be in great danger. Make a note of this curse and turn to 220.

354

Pretending to search through your bag, you clutch the items and mutter the spell. Four coppers materialise in your hand. You hand them to the merchant, who regards them with some suspicion before shrugging and handing over the candle. As you put it in your satchel, he begins prodding you to buy another one.

Make a note of your new possession and turn to 33.

355

With the added luck of the shamrock, your chances of guessing correctly are much higher.

Choose between:

132 213 231

356

You follow the lane to the right, moving quickly in the darkness. Your cloak and boots are soon soaked through with rain. Behind you, the howling wind wreaks a path of destruction, snapping branches and tearing brambles from their roots. You turn into another lane, fighting back the brambles, only to find yourself in a dead end. A shriek fills the air. You press yourself against the stone, straining to hear the wings of the Air Elemental. Will the Darkward spell hold this creature back if you are cornered? Your questions, you realise, are about to be answered. An icy draught of wind heralds the Elemental as it appears; a looming, menacing shape at the end of the lane.

Will you try to dodge the Elemental (turn to **185**), climb the wall (turn to **342**) or combat the creature (turn to 217)?

357

You carve your triangle. Effie expels a breathy grunt as she examines your move. She carves her next cross. You see immediately that she has made a big mistake.

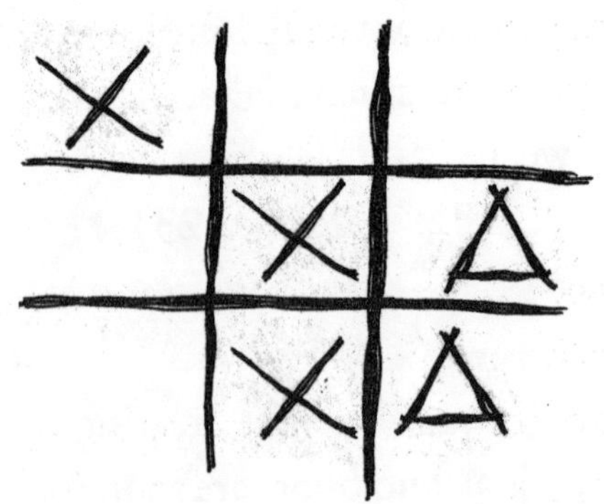

There is only one move you need to make to win three triangles in a row (turn to 75).

358

The merchant regards your offering, shrugs, pulls out a short-handled knife from his coat and saws the bottom of the candle off. He hands you the shortened stub and takes your money. As you put the candle in your satchel, he begins prodding you to buy another one.

Make a note of your new possession and turn to 33.

359

With the luck of the shamrock, you squeeze through the brambles covering the tunnel entrance. The Elemental reaches the tunnel just as you are safely behind the wall of branches and thorns. The creature is bigger than you, and it paces uncertainly, breathing heavily as the rain pours down around it. Wasting no time, you scramble forward in the dark.

The bramble thorns are magical and will not poison you so long as you are protected by the Darkward spell.

Turn to 328.

360

With the luck of the shamrock, you have a greater chance of surviving.

Choose now between the following routes:

Route 1: 155.
Route 2: 338.

361

At length you appeal to Cyleric for help. His mood grows dark.

'The magick of the Elder Fey be nun trifled. If ye can nun answer the riddle, then I will conceade my mistake. For this I be in debt to the Ordughadh, for I have revealed too much of their secretted wayes to a stranger and for my breeche of truste I be bound by honour to silence ye.'

Before you grasp his intent, Cyleric pulls the knife from his cloak and with a deftness that defies his age, he crosses the table and plunges the weapon deep into your stomach. His mark is true; you slump to the floor.

Turn to **368**.

362

You utter the spell. The ring glows hot in your palm and the smell of burning paper rises as the ring transforms into a piece of silvery parchment. Upon it are written the following words:

The Forgotten Spell! You have found it at last. You are now the sole keeper of the ancient and powerful words. You read the spell over again, though you dare not utter the syllables. Your gaze then falls to the envelope, the only other item in the box. You pull it out, reading the poem on the front:

May thee who finds this letter
Unbind the seal that keep it clo'ed
By virtue of thy name and blood
The King's true child be knowen

You turn the envelope over: it is sealed with a non-descript, grey wax. You touch the wax lightly, and to your surprise, it immediately begins to melt. The paper separates and you open the envelope carefully, pulling free a blank page upon which writing immediately begins to appear.

To read the letter, turn to **369**.

363

You pick up the tin. The imp grows aggressive, snatching it off you.

Do you want to wrest it from him (turn to **180**), bribe him for it (turn to **280**) or choose something else (return to **211**)?

364

There is only one thing that will expel the banshee's curse and restore your voice: a potent oil that is extracted from the leaves of the ghoul's thistle.

If you have these leaves in your possession, you may use them now. Otherwise, you must keep an eye out for a cure. Until you find a cure, you will be unable to cast any spells. If you have any other injuries to attend to, return to **165**. Otherwise, turn to **281**.

365

Try as you might, you cannot find the Warlock's name. You glance about, feeling nervous and exposed by the shadows of nightfall. If you cannot enter the Warlock's home, you will have to spend the night in the courtyard. You step back reluctantly from the doorway. As you do, you feel your limbs begin to stiffen. The air is leached from your pores as your skin contracts, pressing down on the tissues and organs inside your body. Your tongue thickens and your windpipe constricts. You try to gasp for breath, but your lungs turn to mortar. For a brief moment there is life behind your eyes before that too is extinguished, as your body is taken by the spell and turned to stone.

Turn to 368.

366

Effie grips her knife in one fleshy, hair-stubbled fist and carves a cross on the table. You hear chuckles and whistles coming from onlookers. Another knife is thrust on the table in front of you. You pick up the grimy handle. From the scratchings of past games, it seems you need to carve a triangle for your move. But where?

X	104	212
28	91	174
115	57	313

Pick your square and turn to the corresponding number.

367

You utter the spell. The words on the plaque change before your eyes to read:

The door be unlocked, friend

What door? The stone wall is solid under your hand, just as it appears to your eye. You inspect it from top to bottom, but can find no magical entrance. You step back, hoping a broader view might reveal the secret, when suddenly you trip on something. You look down to see an iron handle set in the cobblestones.

Excited, you grasp the handle and pull hard. A square area of stones lifts away from the pavement as the door opens. Looking down, you see a set of torchlit, spiral steps leading into the darkness.

Turn to 336.

368

You are dying as you read these words. Death is the fate of a mortal, and you would be dead already if it were not for your heritage, for you carry in your veins the blood of the Elder Fey. As such, you are able to use the power of restoration that is the birthright of all Elder Fey.

THE POWER OF RESTORATION

The power of restoration deems that you can return to the world of the living via a portal in the past. You may invoke this power almost every time you die (with some magical exceptions), but beware! The results are not always favourable. Sometimes you will journey so far into the past that you will have to repeat much of your quest. On the other hand, you may also have the opportunity to find new clues which will help you on your quest. It is all a matter of luck...

During this revitalisation process, all lost power or vitality will return to you, so that you will be fully able to cast spells and combat foes. You will also retain your possessions, no matter at which stage in the journey you collected them.

HOW TO INVOKE THE POWERS OF RESTORATION

You must read the following instructions before carrying them out. Firstly, focus in your mind on a place you wish to return to. Close the book, turn it around three times, then open to a random page. If you clearly recognise any of the paragraphs, then the restoration is complete and you must begin your quest again from that paragraph. If you recognise more than one paragraph, you may choose which one to return to. You may feel a little disoriented for a while, not knowing exactly where you are, but that is a natural part of restoration. Keep reading!

If you do not recognise any of the paragraphs on that page, close the book and repeat the process again.

369

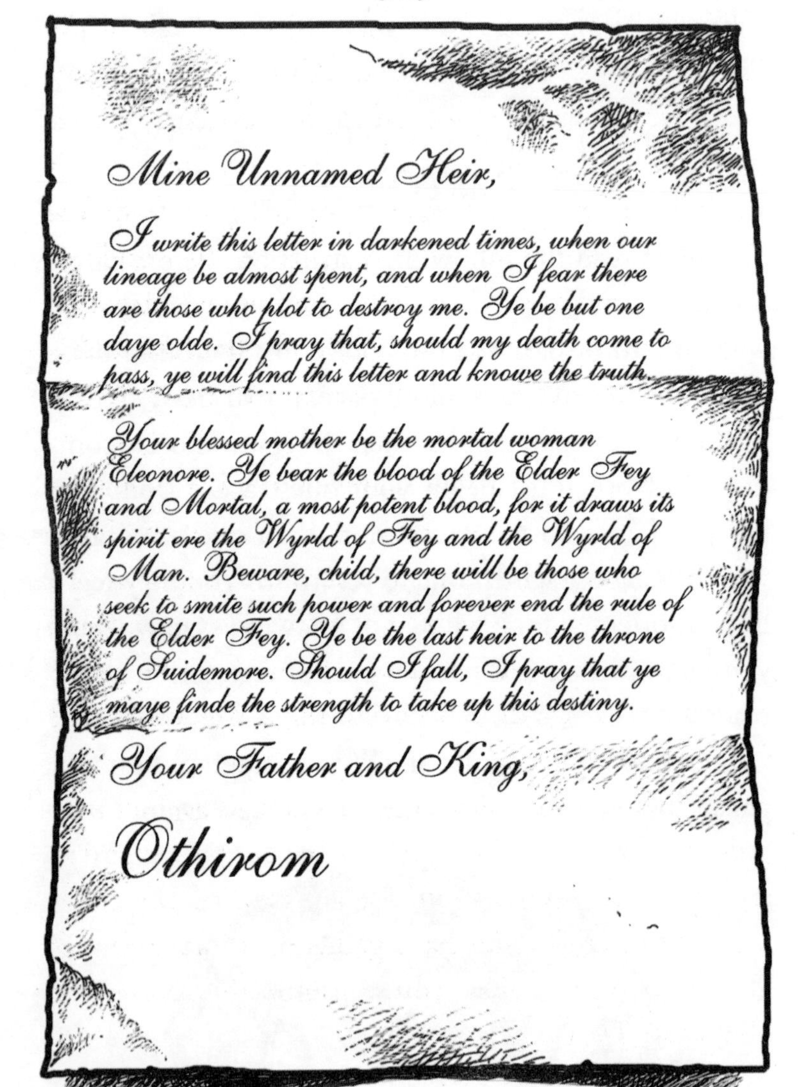
369

Mine Unnamed Heir,

I write this letter in darkened times, when our lineage be almost spent, and when I fear there are those who plot to destroy me. Ye be but one daye olde. I pray that, should my death come to pass, ye will find this letter and knowe the truth.

Your blessed mother be the mortal woman Eleonore. Ye bear the blood of the Elder Fey and Mortal, a most potent blood, for it draws its spirit ere the Wyrld of Fey and the Wyrld of Man. Beware, child, there will be those who seek to smite such power and forever end the rule of the Elder Fey. Ye be the last heir to the throne of Suidemore. Should I fall, I pray that ye maye finde the strength to take up this destiny.

Your Father and King,

Othirom

Turn to 154.

370

Congratulations! You have survived the attack of the Air Elementals and have passed through the ancient portal which will lead you on to the next part of your journey. You have much to be proud of, for your wit and elementary magic have protected you from the pursuit of Olcrada and the servants of his cauldron. Moreover, you have succeeded in finding the Forgotten Spell. With the passing of the Arch Warlock, the spell is now in your charge. Should you lose it, it will be lost forever.

The task that lies ahead is grave indeed. You will be called upon to find your father, the King of the Elder Fey, and revoke the spell. Take heed of the lessons you have learnt, for you will need all your courage and skill to survive the dangers that lie waiting for you in the second part of your journey through Suidemor, the City of the Faery.

Though you have lost all your belongings, you may presume that your coins were kept in your pocket and so are still in your possession. Keep a note of any clues, blessings or curses you have gathered so far. You will need these again when you continue the journey in book two, *The Gatekeeper's Oath*.

The OrdughadH of the
Elder Fey
The EighT SpelS
of
ElementarY EldeR MagiC

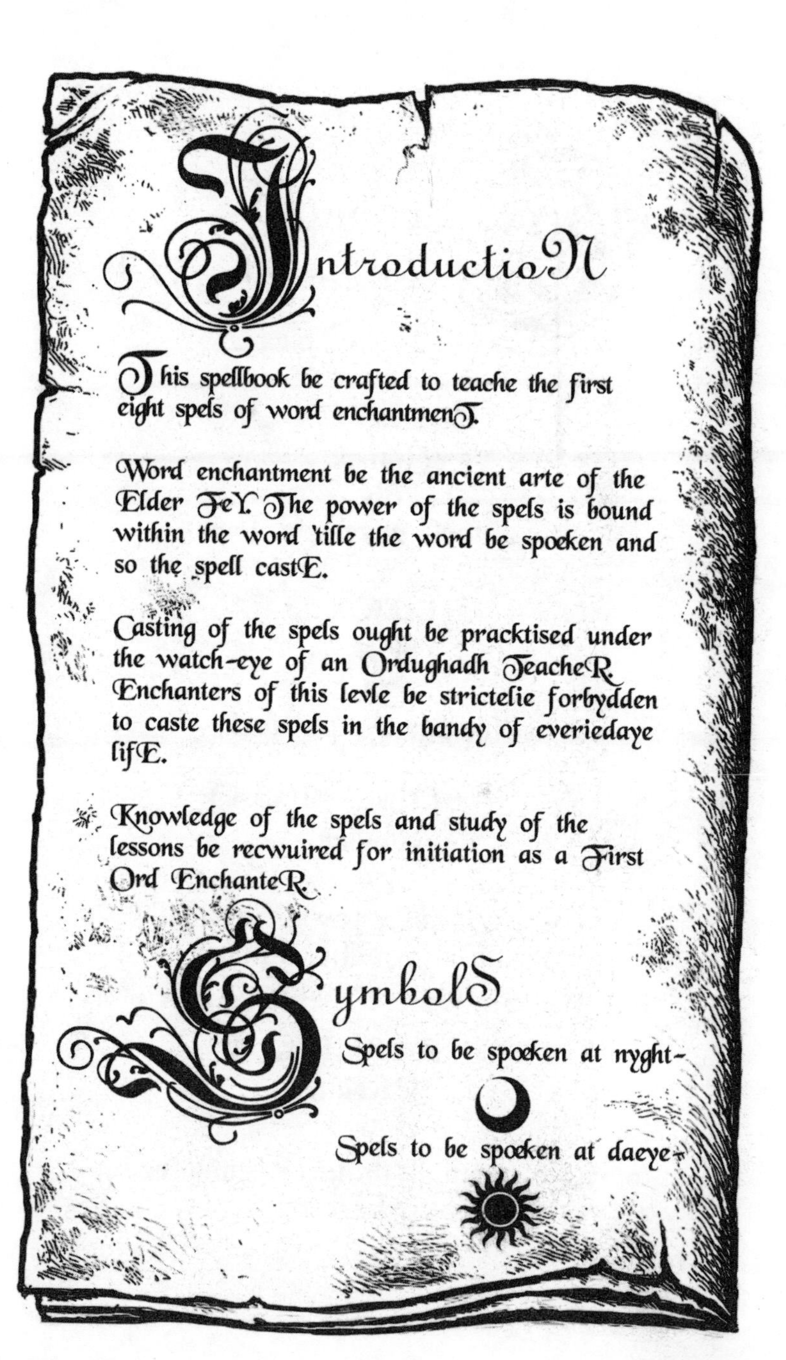

IntroductioN

This spellbook be crafted to teache the first eight spels of word enchantmenT.

Word enchantment be the ancient arte of the Elder FeY. The power of the spels is bound within the word 'tille the word be spoeken and so the spell castE.

Casting of the spels ought be pracktised under the watch-eye of an Ordughadh TeacheR. Enchanters of this levle be strictelie forbydden to caste these spels in the bandy of everiedaye lifE.

Knowledge of the spels and study of the lessons be recwuired for initiation as a First Ord EnchanteR.

SymbolS

Spels to be spoeken at nyght-

Spels to be spoeken at daeye-

ЏDDĿŒЄЖ ☽☀

Unlock

66

to unlock a symple lock

ĿŒЄЖ ☽☀

Lock

32

to lock a symple lock

ŞĿЏMБЭЯ ☽☀

Slumber

73

to warreante a fey or animal
to fall in goodlie slumber
(warreanted nun on magickal beings)

ЯÆŞÆD ☽☀

Raesan

51

to raese a small thing or small being
into the aire

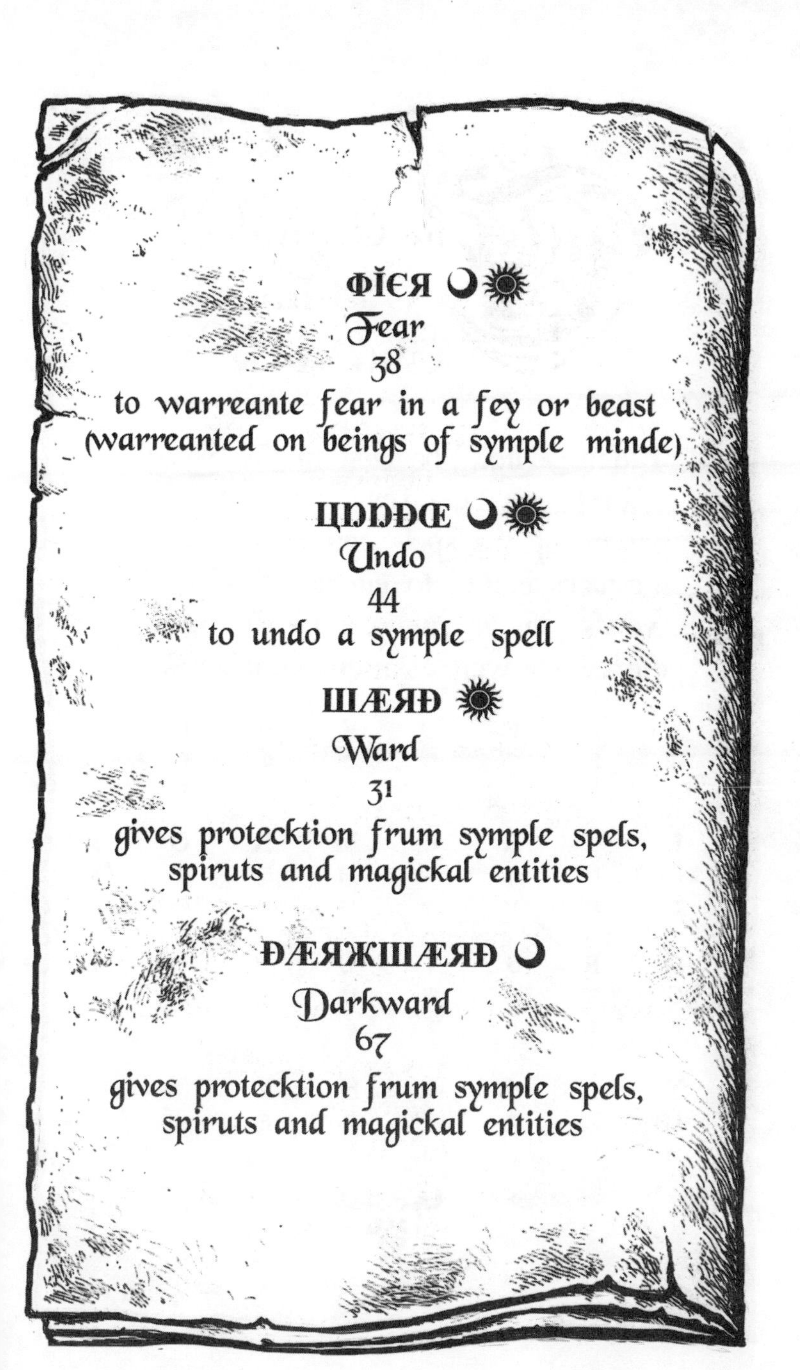

ФЇЄЯ ☽ ☀

Fear

38

to warreante fear in a fey or beast
(warreanted on beings of symple minde)

ЦDDÐŒ ☽ ☀

Undo

44

to undo a symple spell

ШÆЯÐ ☀

Ward

31

gives protecktion frum symple spels,
spiruts and magickal entities

ÐÆЯЖШÆЯÐ ☽

Darkward

67

gives protecktion frum symple spels,
spiruts and magickal entities

ElderMagiC be cast in the Spoeken WorD, an olde fey alphabeT. The power of the spels commes frum the numbers bound to eache letteR. Alle words can be changed into numbers, thence knowen as name-numberS.

A	B	C	D	E	F	G	H
Æ	Б	Є	Đ	Э	Φ	Ґ	Ъ
1	2	3	4	5	6	3	8
I	J	K	L	M	N	O	P
Ĭ	ſ	Ж	Ŀ	M	Ŋ	Œ	þ
7	3	11	12	13	14	6	17
Q	R	S	T	U	V	W	X
Ơ	Я	Ş	Ψ	Ц	V	Ш	X
19	20	15	9	6	6	6	22
Y	z	th	sh	silent H	silent E	silent letters	
Ы	Z	Ђ	Ч	Њ	Ę	all	
10	7	18	21	3	8	16	

PUZZLE SOLVER

The Stone Wall – 70

There are 16 nettle-free stones.

Turn to **16**.

The Bookshop – 113

= 2 (top bookshelf)
= 8 (mirror)
= 4 (front bookshelf)

Turn to **284**.

The Triangle Puzzle – 117

There are 35 triangles.

Turn to 35.

One methodical way of calculating them is by labelling each triangle and then writing down all the combinations, as follows:

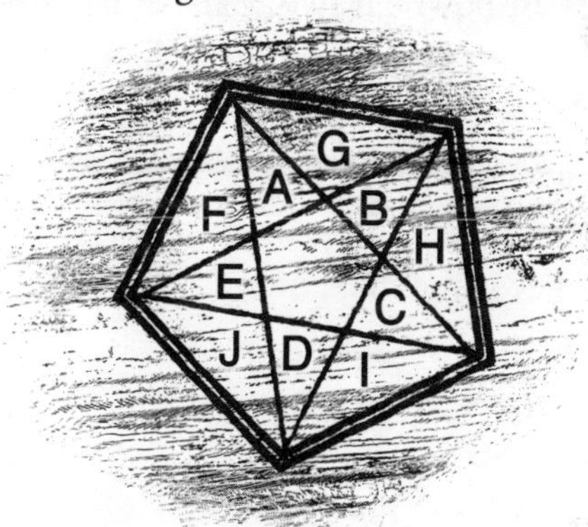

Each set of brackets represents one triangle:

(A) (B) (C) (D) (E) (F) (G) (H) (I) (J) = 10 triangles
(AF) (AG) (AFG) (ADIC) (AC) = 5 triangles
(BG) (BH) (BGH) (BEJD) (BD) = 5 triangles
(CH) (CI) (CHI) (CEFA) (CE) = 5 triangles
(DI) (DJ) (DIJ) (DAGB) (DB) = 5 triangles
(EJ) (EF) (EJF) (EBHC) (EC) = 5 triangles
TOTAL = 35 triangles

Graffiti Puzzle – 299 & 330

There are 8 triangles hidden in the shape.

Turn to 8.

The Arch Warlock's Name – 281

The Arch Warlock's name is hidden upside down in the orange tree. Turn the picture around to find the letters in the branches. If you consult the faery alphabet, you will find that the letters add up to 53.

Turn to 53.

The Bowl Puzzle – 350

Each bowl is identified by the triangles in the pattern around the bowl. The first bowl has two triangles in a row, the second has one and the third has three. The order is therefore 213.

Turn to 213.

Key Puzzle – 172

The matching key is the third one.

Turn to 324.

Key Puzzle – 300

The matching key is the first one.

Turn to 315.

Key Puzzle – 245

The matching key is the third one.

Turn to 322.